EVERYBODY LOVES RAYMOND

OUR FAMILY ALBUM

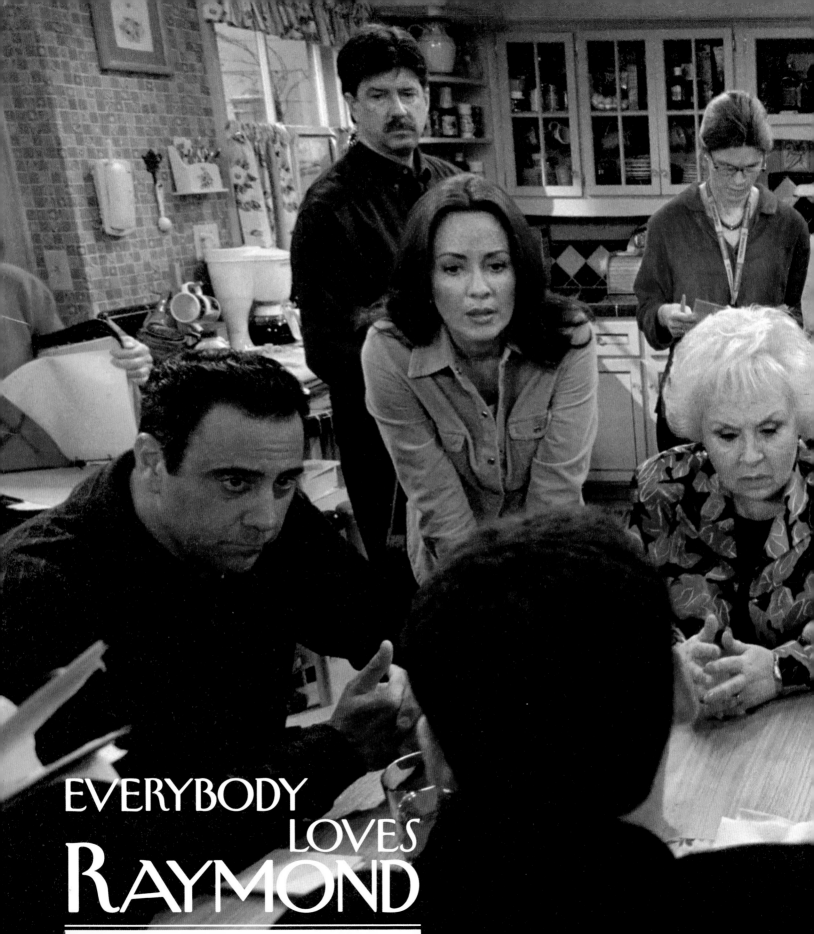

EVERYBODY LOVES RAYMOND

RAY ROMANO & PHIL ROSENTHAL

PHOTOGRAPHY BY TOM CALTABIANO
FOREWORD BY NORMAN LEAR
INTERVIEWS BY HEATHER HAVRILESKY

HBO   WORLDWIDE PANTS   MELCHER MEDIA

This book was produced by Melcher Media, Inc.
124 West 13th Street, New York, NY 10011

Publisher: Charles Melcher
Editor in Chief: Duncan Bock
Project Editors: Megan Worman and David E. Brown
Publishing Manager: Bonnie Eldon
Production Director: Andrea Hirsh

Ray Romano: Thank you to everyone who does anything at all on this show. Success is a good thing, but everyone's great spirit and goodwill are what make this experience unforgettable. Thank you to my family, Anna, Ally, Greg, Matt, and Joe, my mom and dad, and my brothers, Richard and Robert. Thank you to Les Moonves and CBS, Chris Albrecht and HBO, Dave Letterman and Worldwide Pants. Thanks to my agent, Sam Haskell, and to George Savitsky, Gary Satin, Jon Moonves, and my manager of thirteen years, Rory Rosegarten. Thank you to my talented assistant, Christy Kallhovd. Thank you, Richard Marion, your talent matched your heart. Thank you cast and crew, and thank you writers, you're the best there is. Thanks to my friend Tom Caltabiano for the idea of this book and for showing us how eight years of him annoying us with his camera could end up giving us something as worthwhile as this. And thank you, Phil, for being the Jewish version of me, if I was creatively brilliant and it was possible to make my ass even flatter.

Phil Rosenthal: Thanks to everyone who's ever worked on *Everybody Loves Raymond*; all our friends at CBS, Worldwide Pants, and HBO, especially Les Moonves, David Letterman, and Chris Albrecht; every teacher and professor who had to put up with me; all the great shows and show-runners who came before us; Arnold Margolin; Ed Weinberger; Barry Kemp; Monica, Ben, and Lily; my parents; my brother, Richard, and his family; Patti Felker; Adam Berkowitz; Alan Kirschenbaum; Oliver Goldstick; Erin Champion; and, most of all, my friend Raymond. Thanks for the good life.

Tom Caltabiano: I began taking pictures on the set of *Everybody Loves Raymond* because my friend Ray was starring in it. Since most shows get cancelled in the first season, I thought he should have some photos to help him remember the short-lived experience. But the show lasted, and I no longer had one friend on the show, but 130 people who became my family. I hope these photos provide some insight into what it's like to be a part of *Raymond*. This book would not have been possible without Ray and Phil and the cast and crew of *Raymond*. Thanks to Charlie Melcher, David Brown, and Meg Worman for their patience, knowledge, and guidance through the bookmaking process; Cheyenne Pesko, for his endless talents; Valerie DeKeyser for her impeccable design skills; Jon Kunkel and Joe Bevans, my photographic mentors; the writers of *Raymond*, Steven J. Meyer, and Adam Lorenzo for their help with the episode guide; Heather Havrilesky, for her insightful writing and interviews; Amy Thiel for her dedication and tireless help; Charles A. Robinson IV for his loving care with these images; and Elizabeth Van Itallie for translating *Raymond* onto the printed page. Additional thanks to Chris Albrecht, Mike Berlin, Sue Coppa, Jim Dunn, Bill Fine, Vycki Feldhaus, Wendi Goldstein, Herman Leonard, David Letterman, Susan Maljan, Ken Mann, John Martin, Leslie Maskin, Les Moonves, Gigi New, Rory Rosegarten, Russell Schwartz, Ruthanne Secunda, Neal Sharpe, Steve Twersky, Tim Tyler, the Warner Bros. photo lab, Don Weinstein at Photo Impact Hollywood, and David Wilde. Finally, thanks to my sister, Diane, my parents, and all of my friends.

Many thanks to: Ron Broadhurst, Rob Burnett, Bree Conover, Max Dickstein, Adam de Havenon, Martin Felli, David Lombard, Lauren McKennna, John Meils, Lauren Nathan, Richard Oren, Jeff Peters, Jim Peterson, Lia Ronnen, Corey Sabourin, Lindsey Stanberry, Liate Stehlik, Shoshana Thaler, Elizabeth Van Itallie, and Shân Willis

Pocket Books, a division of Simon & Schuster, Inc., 1230 Avenue of the Americas, New York, NY 10020.

Everybody Loves Raymond: Our Family Album

Portions of the interview with Phil Rosenthal on pages 8–11 first appeared in Salon.com, at www.Salon.com. An online version remains in the Salon archives. Reprinted with permission.

Library of Congress Cataloging-in-Publication data is available upon request.

ISBN: 0-7434-9381-8

First Pocket Books hardcover edition May 2004

10 9 8 7 6 5 4 3 2 1

Pocket and colophon are registered trademarks of Simon & Schuster, Inc. For information regarding special discounts for bulk purchases, please contact Simon & Schuster Special Sales at 1-800-456-6798 or business@simonandschuster.com.

Printed in China

CONTENTS

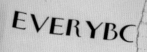

EVERYBO

RAYM

Raymond
..........IST
..."...One"

...............RAY ROMANO
...............PATRICIA HEATON
...............DORIS ROBERTS
...............PETER BOYLE
...............BRAD GARRETT
...............MADYLIN SWEETEN
...............SULLIVAN and SAWYER
SWEETEN

"She's The One"

Written by

Ray Romano
&
Philip Rosenthal

Directed by

John Fortenberry

#0209-713

SHOOTING SCRIPT #4
October 23, 2002

Before I'd ever seen his show, Phil Rosenthal, creator of *Everybody Loves Raymond,* told me that when he was pitching it to the powers that be at CBS, they asked him what kind of show he had in mind. A photograph of the *All in the Family* cast was hanging on the wall in the office where the meeting was taking place. Phil pointed to it. "One like that," he quotes himself as saying. Phil had to be alluding to the success he hoped to have, because to the extent that he intended the show to be like *All in the Family,* he failed. Utterly. Yes, *Everybody Loves Raymond* is about a family. And yes, it is about family life and family relationships, centered around a family member. But the comparison ends somewhere in that neighborhood, because *Everybody Loves Raymond* is a thorough original. Ray Romano's comedy, on which this hit show is based, mined by Rosenthal, its creator, with whom Romano collaborates on an occasional piece, pokes into the nooks and crannies of marriage, family relationships, and human frailty, at levels so deep as to be at once universal and profound.

You don't hear many jokes on *Everybody Loves Raymond.* The laughs come instead from the testing of well-drawn characters in hilariously conceived everyday situations. *Raymond* is not plot-heavy and needn't be, because of the deftness with which the writing and directing probe its characters.

As for the cast, as I've often said of *All in the Family,* of course someone had to make the individual decision to cast each actor. Rosenthal and Romano made those decisions regarding *Raymond.* But who was responsible for each player's being alive and around and at liberty at the exact moment *Raymond* was looking for them? Who was responsible for the talent that likely wasn't visible (perhaps not even available) when the actors were auditioning for their roles; the ripening talent that blossomed over time as a result of the interaction with the other uniquely talented players?

Doris Roberts, Peter Boyle, Patricia Heaton, Brad Garrett—and Ray Romano himself—grew and matured their talents in a nurturing process that is one of the miracles of good theater. And who is responsible for all of that chemistry? No one? Everyone? I'll take the word "miracle" to describe anything that works as well as *Everybody Loves Raymond.*

—NORMAN LEAR

INTRODUCTION
A CONVERSATION WITH RAY ROMANO & PHIL ROSENTHAL

Real families constantly walk a thin line between love and hate, and no show has captured that tightrope walk quite as vividly as *Everybody Loves Raymond.* Sure, there are plenty of truly great family sitcoms, from *The Cosby Show* to *All in the Family,* but the Barones may be the most hauntingly realistic family ever to grace the small screen. With their ambivalence, their petty jealousies, and their misguided attempts at generosity, Ray and his family are thrillingly caustic, unpredictable, and above all, relatable. Instead of floating around in a hopelessly bland sitcom world of sticky sweetness and cloyingly clever comments, Ray and Debra and Marie and the rest do just what we do: They mess up and say stupid things and insult each other and try to fix it, but only make it worse. In other words, they're a family.

While most sitcoms are packed to the brim with shtick that doesn't suit the characters, punch lines that interrupt the action, and ridiculous situations that are as unbelievable as they are uninteresting, *Everybody Loves Raymond* is grounded in interesting, human stories and realistic dialogue. When Ray avoids confronting Debra about her PMS, or Robert tries to win over Amy's incredibly square parents, the laughs are organic and don't require exaggeration. Even the kids act like real kids, instead of bouncing in and out, *Full House*–style, wisecracking and making cute remarks.

More than anything, *Everybody Loves Raymond* is an exploration of the daily trials and tribulations of marriage, and the struggle to accept family members for who they are, no matter how unnerving or impossible they might be. The show portrays the long fall from grace that occurs over the course of a marriage, documenting those painful moments when you're forced to let go of your idealistic, youthful vision of what True Love should look like. One such moment occurs when Robert's future wife, Amy, delivers a rousing speech to Ray, Debra, and Ray's parents on the joys of wedlock: "Robert and I are getting married, and I want us to be honest and trusting, and I hope those feelings will only get stronger the longer that we're together." The couple exits, and after a stunned silence, Ray says, "Wow." Debra turns to him and says nostalgically, "Yeah. Remember when we were that stupid?"

The ability of *Everybody Loves Raymond* to capture the ambivalence and confusion of family life begins and ends with two people: creator Phil Rosenthal and star Ray Romano. By tapping into their families' particular flavors of crazy, these two have created an exasperating but lovable cast of characters and an absolutely unhinged, unforgettable show that will feel real and funny and oddly familiar for generations to come.

Everybody Loves Raymond is so different from the empty slapstick of most of the sitcoms that are on right now. How do you do it?

Phil: It's a character-driven sitcom, as opposed to a joke-driven sitcom. When we first started in 1996, *Seinfeld* was still on, and *Seinfeld* was a great show. I always say that the only thing that was wrong with *Seinfeld* were all the shows that tried to imitate it. I couldn't have done one of those kinds of shows if I wanted to. The shows I grew up with were *The Honeymooners, All in the Family, The Mary Tyler Moore Show, The Dick Van Dyke Show, The Odd Couple,* and *Taxi.* They were all character-based sitcoms, where the humor comes from character, and the story comes from character, and there *is* a story.

Originally, one of the comments I got from one of the studio people was: "I don't understand the type of show you're trying to do here." I said, "I'll tell you. We're trying to do a traditional, well-made, classic type of sitcom." And he said, "All words we should be avoiding." And I said, "And what words should we be going for?" And he said, "Hip and edgy." And I said, "Listen, you got the right guy, because I am Mr. Hip and Edgy."

Hip and edgy, meaning superficial and contrived. *Raymond,* on the other hand, feels like an honest reflection of real lives.

Phil: We have a couple of rules on the show. Probably the main one is, "Could this happen?" You want to stretch credibility as far as you can without destroying the reality, or the thing that people relate to when they watch. You want to take it to the edge, but you don't want to go over. Otherwise you wind up with one of the many shows that I don't need to mention. Silly things happen, and then they have to top themselves because that's all they have.

I think I speak for both of us when I say that everything on this show—everything, including all the success we've had—can be directly attributed to our families.

Ray: And our writers. And their families.

Phil: The genesis for everything on the show comes from experiences with our parents and our wives. It was Ray's actual life.

Ray: The actual setting—you know, parents across the street, brother is a police officer living in his parents' house—that was all happening. My brother was a divorced cop who moved back in with my parents, who lived nearby. CBS wanted them in the house, and for the brother to be a security guard, not a cop. They wanted the wife to be more blond, middle-American—not ethnic. They wanted my last name not to end with a vowel.

Phil: So we fooled them with Barone. It still ends with an "e," but it's a silent "e."

Ray: It was originally going to be set in Queens, where I'm from. But they didn't want the city. They gave us Long Island.

Phil: We compromised with Long Island. Five minutes away, literally. Queens is here, Long Island is here. Queens is attached to Long Island! Still, I'd say that 90 percent of what you see on that show happened to me, or to Ray, or to one of the other writers. And we take it from there, until the characters start to have their own lives.

Ray: In fact, the title of the show comes from something my brother said. He used to jokingly begrudge the situation where he has to chase criminals for a living and everybody hates him and he gets paid very little money. And look at Raymond: He grows up, and everybody loves Raymond. He used to say, "Everybody loves Raymond! Look at Raymond!" And so we used that as the working title.

Phil: My wife saw it in the script and said, "That should be the title of the show." Ray hated it.

Ray: I hated it.

Phil: Anyone would hate a show called "Everybody Loves . . ." with their name there. That's like inviting people to hit you on the head. I totally understood.

Ray: I tried to change it. Even Phil said, "When the time comes, we'll change it."

Phil: And I meant it.

Ray: I talked to the head of CBS, Les Moonves. I said, "Listen, Les. This show is going to be a top ten show, and I'm going to have to live with that title for the rest of my life." I was trying to appeal to him with humor. And he said, "Ray, if this show is top fifteen, you can change it to whatever you want." And in the second or third year it was top

fifteen, and he's like, "You can't change it now."

Phil: Of course!

Ray: I have something hanging in my dressing room, because I was just obsessing over this, a scrap of paper with all the possible names we could use [see page 11]. Les Moonves said, "Give me something better." So I tried to come up with something and he tested them with an audience, and he reported back, "'Everybody Loves Raymond' was the highest." And I said, "That's why you shouldn't use it." I have that list framed. You look at the list, and it looks like it's a joke. It's a scrap of paper with names like "Raymond's Tree"—you know, because of the family tree? "That Raymond Guy." And there's one that says, "Um, Raymond."

How was the first year on the air? Were you nervous about getting axed?
Phil: Well, we started out on Friday

nights. Once the show took off, in March of the first year, they moved us to Mondays, and our ratings doubled.

Ray: But it was a little bit of a test. It was a little bit of, "If we don't perform here, then we could be on the chopping block."

Phil: I was most nervous after that first Monday night. I thought, "Oh, so we got sampled Monday. Next week we're going to drop, and that's it." And it was that next week when the ratings went up, I think. When that happened, I kept this. [Pulls small piece of paper from his wallet.] It's a clipping from *Variety*.

Ray: Oh, really? [Reads clipping] "On Monday of this week, *Everybody Loves Raymond* has probably clinched a permanent berth in the CBS Monday lineup."

Phil: That's when I knew we'd made it.

Ray: "*Raymond* improved by its best yet, 24

percent on its 18–49 lead-in from *Cosby*."

Phil: That right there is why we're sitting here.

Ray: [Still looking at the clipping] *Cosby* was a rerun! It says "rerun."

Phil: He'll always find the negative. *Cosby* was a rerun, so of course we were going to go up. See, that's what he's thinking. It's such a pleasure. There was another scare during the third season, when they said, "*Raymond* is now going to move to 9 p.m. Mondays," up against the most popular show in America at the time, *Monday Night Football*, and the other most popular show, *Ally McBeal*. So I thought, "This is where we tank. This is the end now." And then, within a few months, we were beating both of them. We still beat *Monday Night Football* every week.

Ray: Well, *Monday Night Football* doesn't

get the ratings it used to. That's why.

One thing that makes *Everybody Loves Raymond* different from other sitcoms is that the jokes never seem to interrupt the flow of action.
Phil: If they do, we take them out. We work on the jokes last. We're also not afraid of dramatic moments.

Did you integrate drama into the show from the beginning?
Phil: Yeah. I truly believe dramatic moments help to strengthen the characters, and make it funnier when those characters do something. Like on *The Honeymooners*, I remember one episode where Norton got hurt after a fight with Ralph. Norton is the funniest character ever on television. All he ever did was make you laugh, and if he's hurt—oh my God! Your heart breaks for him. And then you see how it affects Ralph. He rushes to the hospital to give a transfusion, and of course Norton is fine, but Ralph has to give the blood anyway. You just laugh harder because, suddenly, they're more real as people. It's a heartier laugh, not a surface laugh. We believe them as human beings.

Listen, how many chances do you get to have your own TV show, right? You can have something that succeeds in the short term—you gotta make 'em laugh at every second, you gotta have ten laughs per page or they're gonna turn the channel—or you can try to make something that might have lasting value. The best advice I ever got from an old show-runner was, "Do the show you want to do, because in the end they're gonna cancel you anyway."

Ray: We don't do dramatic moments very often, but when we do, it's earned, and it's short, and it's sweet. I didn't want to do a show that had special episodes or heavy moments. But the right dramatic moment is real, and it helps the comedy.

The sets of many sitcoms are reported to be wildly dysfunctional, but yours is rumored to have one of the friendliest working environments in TV.

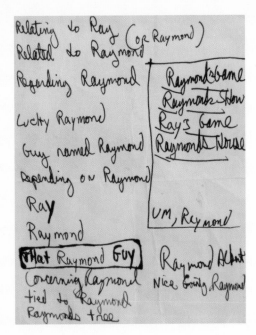

Phil: I think it's the food. The name of my production company is Where's Lunch? That's the writers' main preoccupation. So the food has to be very good, because when you're in a room all day, the only sunshine that comes in is the menu.

So has everybody gained about ten pounds per season?
Phil: Yeah, now we're all trying to lose it. We're a very happy group, and we do things together outside of work. Yesterday we all went to the Lakers game. We have a great time. Nothing is taken for granted.

We understand how rare this is. We're living in the moment and enjoying it, and I hope that comes through. I hope a spirit of fun is underneath all the apparent discord.

You push the boundaries of likability for each character, yet they all remain likable.
Phil: Likability is a funny word. The network always wants the characters to be likable. To which I say, "Who in your family do you really like?" To me, people are likable if they make me laugh.

Ray: Look at Danny DeVito in *Taxi*. Mean character, but you love him.

How have you managed to set the bar so high all these years?
Phil: I tell people we're trying to be the Bruce Springsteen of sitcoms. When you go to a Springsteen concert, it's the best time you've ever had, the most fun you've ever had, and yet you leave with something. It might be an emotional moment or something powerful that happened, but you're left with something. You identified with and were connected to something larger than your own experience. Something that stays with you. It's because we're here for a short time, not just life, but our sitcom life. We have a chance to make our mark, right? So why not make that count?

RAY ROMANO BEFORE RAYMOND

The middle child of three sons, Ray Romano was born on December 21, 1957, to Albert, an engineer, and Lucie, a piano teacher, in the Forest Hills section of Queens, New York. From early on, Ray showed signs of comedic leanings and rampant self-deprecation, when, as a teenager, he formed a sketch group with his friends called No Talent, Inc., which performed in the basement of a local church. While he got kicked out of two high schools before graduating from a third, Ray's comedic talent was never in question. "He was always very funny. He was always cuckoo," reports younger brother Robert.

Ray's family's hopes for him may have dimmed slightly when he quit Queens College after accumulating only fifteen credits in three years. "He went to work at a gas station, and during that year and a half he was robbed at gunpoint twice," Lucie recalls. "The second time, we said, 'That's it, get out.'" After this run-in with reality, Ray returned to Queens College and suddenly became a stellar student, making the Dean's List for three years while studying accounting.

Ray began appearing in local comedy clubs and quit school (again) his senior year to dedicate himself to stand-up. He worked a wide variety of jobs to make ends meet, from futon deliveryman to bank teller. In 1985, Ray met Anna, who was a teller at the same bank, and the two were soon married. A couple of years later, Ray decided to pursue stand-up comedy full-time.

After winning a local comedy contest sponsored by a New York radio station in 1989, Ray signed with a manager, Rory Rosegarten, and began to get national attention. "As a comic, you watched Johnny Carson and dreamed," he remembers. In 1991, Ray's dream came true when he was asked to appear on *The Tonight Show.* "The day of the show, I went into the shower," Ray says. "And I remember thinking, 'Okay, this is the shower I'm taking before I'm on the

Johnny Carson show.' And my arm felt numb. I couldn't feel my arm! Then I started to get *really* nervous—not for the show, but because I was getting so nervous. By the time I got into the limo, I was thinking, 'I am a mess. This is not gonna work!'"

After the show, Carson came by to congratulate him. "He shook my hand and said, 'You gotta like that!' Then Ed McMahon came in: 'Ho ho ho! Good

job!' It was cool." Ray's timing was impeccable—Carson retired just four months later.

After continuing to do stand-up for three more years, Ray was cast as the handyman on *News Radio*—only to be kicked off the show after one day. "Pretty quickly, I knew that I was not cutting it," Ray says. "Sure enough, at 6:30 the next morning, the phone rang, and it was Rory. As soon as he said 'Hello,' I knew. He said the usual Hollywood thing: 'They're going in another direction.'"

Ray was disappointed at the time. "The character just didn't feel organic to me. I felt that I was forcing it." But as his brother Richard so memorably said, "It never ends for Raymond!" Within months, Ray was asked to appear on *Late Night with David Letterman.*

Ray's six-minute appearance on *Late Night* in 1995 so impressed the host and impresario that Letterman approached him about developing a sitcom for Letterman's production company, Worldwide Pants.

Two months later, Ray flew out to Los Angeles to meet with potential writers, and found himself across the table from Phil Rosenthal. "We met at Art's Deli," Phil recalls, "'Where every sandwich is a work of Art.' That's their motto."

After meeting with about a dozen writers, Ray narrowed it down to two he thought were a good fit.

"I was the second choice," Phil says.

"Yeah, Phil and another guy," Ray recalls. "And the other guy was busy!"

PHIL ROSENTHAL BEFORE RAYMOND

Born in Queens, New York, to Helen and Max Rosenthal, Phil Rosenthal's first passion was for acting. His mother says that he knew he wanted to be an actor from the time he was four years old—which is grounds for round-the-clock observation by a child psychologist in most states. Instead, like many kids of the era, Phil spent a great deal of time in front of the television set, watching *The Dick Van Dyke Show* and *All in the Family* with an intensity that made his parents worry for his future.

Phil was a distracted student in high school, but focused on being a comedian in his school's plays. After graduating from Hofstra University in 1981, Phil moved to New York City to dedicate himself to acting full-time. His parents were supportive of his choice. "I always had a very important safety net in them," he reports. "So if I was going to be an actor in New York, which is a stupid thing to do, they weren't going to let me starve."

Phil wasn't so stupid that he ignored opportunity when it came knocking. Alan Kirschenbaum, a close friend of Phil's from high school, showed up at his door one day with a word processor and an idea for a screenplay. The two collaborated on a script about a suburban detective from Rockland County, New York, where they both grew up. A few months later, HBO bought the script.

Phil's luck continued in 1986, when he attended a play starring Monica Horan, a fellow Hofstra graduate and New York City thespian. He was so impressed by her performance that he sent a boldly flirtatious note backstage: "Tell that girl that she's really funny." Monica was smitten, but it took Phil two full weeks to ask her

out, and four years to marry her.

Despite his luck selling scripts and wooing women, Phil remained determined to follow the path of the starving actor. Thus, when an agent saw Phil in a play in New York and reportedly told him afterwards, "If you come to L.A., you'll never stop working as an actor," Phil packed his bags. "Like a schmuck, I moved to L.A., and I

never *started* working as an actor."

He couldn't catch a break as an actor, but Phil's writing talent was obvious to almost everyone who encountered his work. His old friend Alan had broken into sitcoms and was writing for a show in L.A., so Phil teamed up with writer and friend Oliver Goldstick and wrote two spec scripts. They gave the scripts to Alan's agent, Adam Berkowitz, who had represented Phil and Alan on their screen-

play. The two were signed by the William Morris Agency within a week.

Still, as anyone with experience in television can tell you, the only thing tougher than breaking in is getting on a show that sticks around for more than one season. Phil and Oliver's first job was writing for a sitcom called *A Family for Joe,* starring Robert Mitchum. "You don't really put him at the top of the list for sitcom stars," Phil says. "But I loved him." Most of the other writers on the show weren't familiar with Mitchum's work, so Phil invited them over to his apartment to watch *Night of the Hunter.* "They all kind of laughed at it, and I thought, 'Oh, this is gonna be a bumpy road.'" The show lasted seven episodes.

After short stints on *Baby Talk* (the sitcom adaptation of *Look Who's Talking*) and a Ray Sharkey sitcom called *The Man in the Family,* Phil and Oliver joined the writing staff of *Down the Shore,* a show about three girls and three guys sharing a beach house, created by Phil's old friend Alan Kirschenbaum. The show was only on the air for two years, but it was produced by HBO Independent Productions, which later brought Phil into the mix in the early stages of developing *Everybody Loves Raymond.*

After *Down the Shore,* Phil joined the writing staff of *Coach.* During his third year with the show, he saw a new comedian, Ray Romano, performing on *Letterman* one night. "I just happened to be watching that night, and I said, 'Oh, that guy's really funny,'" says Phil. "And then I forgot about it."

But not for long. Two months later, he got a tape of Ray from his agent, with news that the comedian was looking for a writer to help him create a sitcom.

MAKING THE PILOT

THE PREMISE

From their first meeting, Phil and Ray easily found common ground. "We were both from Queens, it turned out," Ray says. "We talked about our parents, and for every story I had, he had one."

"It was 'Can You Top This' with crazy parents," Phil reports. The more they talked, the more Phil began to think that Ray's family should form the basis for the sitcom. "He tells me about his parents living close by in Queens, that they lived with his brother, who's a cop, who's older, who's divorced, who eats by touching every bite of food to his chin before he puts it in his mouth, and is jealous of Raymond and says, when he sees Raymond's Cable Ace Award for Comedy, 'It never ends for Raymond. Everybody loves Raymond.'"

Not only was Ray's family strange and interesting in very specific ways, but casting Ray in a familiar setting made practical sense. "Here's a guy who never acted before," Phil recalls. "I'm gonna make him something close to what he is. I'm not gonna make him a gay astronaut from Cleveland."

Phil also recognized that by focusing on family in the show, he could explore his own family's dynamics. "I thought, 'What a great opportunity for me to get out some of the stories of my family, and the personalities of my family.' It's kind of an amalgam of our two backgrounds."

WRITING

Once they settled on a focus for the sitcom, Phil had to figure out a plot for the pilot. A lot was riding on that first episode. Not only did it have to sell the network on the show, but it would set the tone for the entire series.

"We went in to pitch the show," Phil recounts, "and I said, 'You like Ray? That's pretty much the show. His personality. His family. What he's dealing with.'

And nobody's jumping up and down. They're not saying, 'Wow, a guy who lives across the street from his parents!' They were looking for something more exciting. That was the year that a lot of shows with big stars were being picked up. It was [president of CBS] Les Moonves's first scheduling year. He liked our show, and he was very supportive."

In addition to the elements pulled from Ray's family, the pilot featured a scene straight out of Phil's relationship with his mother. He had signed her up for the

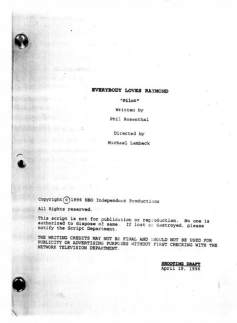

Fruit-of-the-Month Club, and instead of being grateful, she was horrified. "When I got the fruit, there was so much of it," Helen Rosenthal explains, sounding overwhelmed even at the memory. "I'm always afraid of things spoiling. I said, 'Philip, there's so much fruit!'"

"I got that phone call about how terrible it was that I would do this to her," Phil says. "As if I sent plutonium to the house."

A story about how Debra wanted to celebrate her birthday without Ray's parents for a change, and Phil's Fruit-of-the-Month debacle combined to make a memorable first script. "I feel like we hit the ground running, in that we based the

characters on real people," Phil says. "We based them on our families, so they were delineated before we started. Which is a plus—you're not just writing abstractly. You're writing, 'My mother says this!'"

CASTING

Phil: Les Moonves had the idea of casting Peter Boyle for the father. And I said, "Well, I don't think you say no to Peter Boyle." So he came and scared us and we gave him the part.

Ray: He didn't even have to read.

Phil: He was upset that day. He had his family with him, it was hot, he got bad directions, he couldn't find us, and he comes in the door . . . Now, I knew him as the monster in *Young Frankenstein,* and worse, Joe [from the movie *Joe*]. Joe kills kids! So here I am, this punk, and here's Ray—nobody knows who the hell we are. And here's Peter Boyle. He's a movie star.

Ray: What about Doris?

Phil: We saw about a hundred women. We flew back and forth from L.A. to New York, but nobody came close to Doris. Doris hit it out of the park. The Fruit-of-the-Month Club story? Doris must have known my family. She nailed it. There wasn't even a close second.

Ray: Robert's character was based on my brother Richard, who was a cop. He's bitter, a funny kind of bitter. But he never spoke the way Brad Garrett delivered that line, real slow and beaten down: "Everybody loves Raymond." This morose kind of a thing.

Phil: Well, when we were casting it, we were thinking maybe someone shorter than Ray as the older brother, who literally has to look up to Raymond. We thought that seemed funny. And then Brad Garrett walks in, and we're like, "That's another way to go . . ." And then he spoke, and we dropped dead laughing. There was no contest. That character is the best example of the actor bringing his own thing to the show and us just going with it. Right away, Ray and Brad had a rapport. They're both hilarious, and they both do stand-up. Brad was the first $100,000 winner for comedy on *Star Search.*

Ray: The first year of *Star Search,* back with Ed McMahon.

Phil: He's been an established comic since he was nineteen. As a kid, he opened for Sinatra and Sammy Davis, Jr., in Vegas.

Ray: Debra was probably the most crucial casting choice we had to make. We saw a lot of women, and we were very close to deciding on Maggie Wheeler, right?

Phil: We loved Maggie. But Ray's already "ethnic." CBS said the wife shouldn't be ethnic. The network had an idea of somebody for the wife, a pretty blond. Try to imagine the show that way. I got a call from one of Les Moonves's underlings: "Les wants So-and-So." I said, "She's totally wrong." And he said, "No, no, no. You didn't hear me. You are nobody, and Les wants So-and-So. If you would like your show on the air, then you will cast So-and-So, or you don't have a show."

Ray: Nice.

Phil: So I was going to quit, that's how important the role was. Debra has to be

funny, sexy, vulnerable, tough, smart— everything Ray's going up against. But I agreed to let So-and-So read.

Ray: She just wasn't right. She was not right.

Phil: It would've become like *Bridget Loves Bernie.* Like this wife is a fish out of water, the only blond in a sea of Italian people. She meets with us, and I'm told that Les is going to get up at the network auditions and say, "What about So-and-So?" And if I don't say "Yes," I'm dead. So I'm very nervous, and that morning, So-and-So reads for me, and she is lovely and charming and ten times worse than I thought she'd be.

Ray: Worse for the part.

Phil: So now I don't know what I'm going to do. I guess I have to quit. At CBS that afternoon, right on cue, Les says, "What about So-and-So?" And I say, "I think she's great. I've loved her in everything she's done and I met with her today and I fell in love with her. I wanted to marry her. But then she read for me, and I have to tell you, it's just not what I wrote. I just don't buy them as a couple. Could she do it? Maybe. But also, maybe, we could do better." And Les says, "It was just an idea."

I learned so much from that. One is, be deferential to the head of anything. Two is, the guy who told me, "Les wants So-and-So, and if you don't use her

you're dead"? He was playing corporate politics. And he's not even there anymore. So don't listen to just anybody. And a week later Patty Heaton walks into the office. She reads once. We saw two hundred girls. Two hundred looking for the right person! She came in and read with Ray. I think she even kissed him in the scene. She was the only one to do that.

Ray: They all kissed me, but she kissed me on the lips!

Phil: That right away sealed it. Because she's a great actress who will actually kiss Ray. It's nice when a great actress comes in. She's the best—and I mean this as the most sincere compliment—the best wife on television.

Ray: The humor, she plays it just right. We wanted the humor and dialogue on the show to be real and to sound natural. Like a real conversation. Patty was perfect.

Phil: I'll tell you the punch line to the story. We shoot the pilot. It goes very well. Well enough to get picked up to go to series, right? So I get the phone call from my agent: "Congratulations, you're going to series. They just want to know who's going to run the show." So I said, "Oh, I assumed me." "They said you never ran a show before. This is a multi-million dollar investment, they're not going to entrust it to you." "So what's going to happen?" "They'll bring in an experienced show-runner over you." And I said, "No, I'm not going to work for somebody else on my own show. I'm writing about my family. We know what

we're doing here." He said, "Okay, let me make a call. Don't get upset." He makes a call, and calls back: "Okay, here's what they'll do. They'll bring in somebody with you, a co-show-runner who's had experience. Makes sense, right?" I said, "Oh, since you put it that way, I quit." This is my lesson to anyone reading this book: Always quit.

Ray: "There's no chicken in this salad? Okay, I quit!"

Phil: So I hung up the phone. And a day goes by, and that day is filled with me thinking, "I've thrown my show away. They picked it up, they got a pilot out of me. They don't need me anymore." My agent called back the next day and said, "Ah, Les is going to let you run the show." I said, "Why?" "He said he liked how you handled that thing with So-and-So."

FILMING

After the countless struggles involved in conceiving the premise of the show, writing it, grappling with input from so many different sources, and finding the perfect cast, the pilot filming not only went smoothly, but gave the whole cast, crew, and staff a feeling that they had created a very promising show.

"The pilot filming went great," Phil recalls. "And there was kind of a calm confidence that we had. I wasn't really nervous because, where I was coming from as a writer, I knew that, if nothing else, I had that Fruit-of-the-Month scene that seemed to work. And Ray and the cast were fantastic."

The style and focus of the pilot set the

perfect tone for the show. "I learned something valuable," Phil says. "You write very specifically because we all deal in specifics. Even if a storyline is not *your* specific, you have something with your parents where you know what that feels like. When you write generally, you miss everybody. It turns out that the universal thing is in the very, very specific detail.

"In the writers' room, we write about and talk about what makes us laugh, and we figure if that works, then maybe we'll hit some other people with the same sense of humor. We're not writing about your family, or trying to. We don't know how to do that. We don't live with you and your family. We live with our families, and that seems to be enough."

Tony Esparza

EPISODE 2
I Love You

PHIL: OUR FIRST EPISODE AFTER THE PILOT. THESE ARE DIFFERENT TWINS THAN IN THE PILOT — THE ORIGINALS HAD GOTTEN TOO BIG, AND THESE BOYS, SAWYER AND SULLIVAN SWEETEN, ARE THE REAL-LIFE SIBLINGS OF OUR ALLY, MADYLIN SWEETEN. THEY WERE SO SMALL AT THE TIME, RAY WASHED THEM BOTH IN THE KITCHEN SINK IN THIS EPISODE.

Ray: In the beginning, Phil and I thought of issues from our lives that could turn into stories. Never being able to say "I love you," unfortunately, is too true in my life. Fortunately, Phil was able to write a great episode about it. I love him.

19

EPISODE 3
I WISH I WERE GUS

PHIL: JEAN STAPLETON SAW THE PILOT AND AGREED TO DO OUR THIRD EPISODE. EDITH BUNKER IS ONE OF THE GREATEST CHARACTERS IN THE HISTORY OF TELEVISION, AND WE TOOK JEAN'S PARTICIPATION IN OUR LITTLE WOODEN SHOW AS A SIGN FROM ABOVE.

Ray: Jean Stapleton was our first guest star, playing Marie's sister, Alda. I remember thinking that week, "How long am I going to be able to pretend I know what I'm doing around these great actors?"

EPISODE 8
IN-LAWS

PHIL: LOOK AT THIS CASTING. OUR CASTING DIRECTOR, LISA MILLER KATZ, HAS ALWAYS DONE A TERRIFIC JOB, AND THE CASTING OF KATHERINE HELMOND AND ROBERT CULP AS DEBRA'S PARENTS IS PERFECT. THEY'RE LOOSELY BASED (LOOSELY!) ON MY BROTHER'S IN-LAWS, WHO REALLY DO VACATION IN VIETNAM. AFTER THIS EPISODE, MY MOTHER CALLED ME: "ARE YOU OUT OF YOUR MIND? WE HAVE TO SEE THESE PEOPLE!"

EPISODE 12
THE BALL

PHIL: I THOUGHT RAY SHOULD GO OVER AND KISS HIS DAD ON THE FOREHEAD AND SAY, "MERRY CHRISTMAS, DAD." RAY SAID, "THAT WOULD NEVER, EVER HAPPEN. NEVER! I'M NOT DOING IT." THAT WAS ONE OF THE FEW TIMES I EVER TOOK AN ACTOR ASIDE. I SAID, "LISTEN, DON'T DO IT. I DON'T WANT YOU TO DO IT. JUST PROMISE ME ONE THING. I'M NOT GONNA MENTION IT AGAIN, BUT COME FRIDAY NIGHT, IF YOU'RE IN THE MOMENT, AND YOU FEEL IT, TRY IT, OKAY?" AND WE GOT TO FRIDAY NIGHT, AND THAT MOMENT — I'M TELLING YOU, IT'S JUST A SITCOM, BUT THERE WASN'T A DRY EYE IN THE HOUSE.

Ray: This is not what I meant when I told Phil I wanted more kissing scenes.

AN INTERVIEW WITH RAY ROMANO

Curiously, when a man becomes a husband, he leaves much of the generosity, hard work, and self-respect of his youth far behind. Ray Barone embodies this transformation, embracing those simple things that so many family men hold dear: a comfortable couch, a good game on TV, and a delightful assortment of snacks within easy reach. Thus, when the wife comes around, as she so often does, looking for a little help with the cleaning or with the kids, or maybe just complaining about complicated stuff that's probably just a symptom of PMS, Ray does what so many other upstanding men might do: He hides under the bed and waits for her to scram. This maneuver frees up his time for more important things, like pizza and golf.

And yet, somehow, the more Ray flinches or sticks his foot in his mouth or weasels his way out of stuff, the more everybody loves him. Ray Romano may hate to be known as the guy whom everybody loves, but he readily admits to possessing the same chameleon-like traits

as his character. He also claims that, unlike his character, he knows when to shut up and follow his wife's orders. While this isn't too hard to believe, given the fact that he's been married for sixteen years, Ray also says that he's smarter than his character, and that they smell the same.

You write for the show and perform on it. How do you balance the two?
I can't be in the room with the writers when I'm rehearsing, obviously. But whenever I'm not rehearsing, I'm in there with them.

It's remarkable that you can do both, since you're in almost every scene.
Last week, there was one scene I wasn't in, and that was the first one of this year. I didn't know what to do with myself.

That's crazy.
Yeah, they don't pay me enough to . . . No, wait a minute. They do.

How does the process of making a show work?

First, someone will come up with an idea. The other day, I went home to my wife, Anna, and my kids, and about ten minutes in, I said to Anna, "Hey, you got a haircut!" My daughter started laughing and said, "You were wrong, Ma!" I said, "What?" And she said, "Mom bet that you wouldn't notice her haircut." So I brought that into the writers' room, and we thought, "This is a good starting point, but where can it go? What can it do?" It evolved into a story about how she's poisoning the kids against me. She's bonding with the kids about how lame I am!

In what ways are you similar to Ray Barone, and in what ways are you different?
Smell, it's just purely smell.

You two smell the same?
Believe it or not, I'm smarter than my character. You wouldn't think so from talking to me. We have a running thing in the writers' room about who's dumber, me or my character. I think overall he's a good person. I hope I'm a good person. But I think he's—not much!—but a little bit more immature and a little bit more selfish than me. We're similar in a lot of ways. On the show, every situation and every reaction is exaggerated a little bit for comedy. I think our underlying feelings in every situation are probably the same.

How similar is your character's marriage to your own relationship with Anna?
In real life, I'm smart enough to know things I can and can't say to my wife, even though I want to. I feel the same things my character does, but I don't act on them.

I think that's probably one of the appeals of the character. Women suspect that if their husbands were really honest, this is what they would get.

What motivates Ray on the show?
I think he just doesn't want any trouble. He wants to keep the peace between his wife and his mother. He doesn't want to work any more than he has to, I know that. He's lazy. He loves the kids, but he'd rather watch a game with them than take them to the park. He wants it easy, you know?

Do you have a trick for getting into character?
When the show started, the goal was just to make this character me. That's the way it started, and then Ray slowly evolved into his own person. It's very subtle, but he is not me.

In other words, it's like you've evolved this alternate personality.
Yes, and you know, we've done it for eight years now. It's almost subconscious, to act like Ray Barone. I just snap into it—it's a mannerism, it's a way of carrying myself, it's a very slight dumbing down of myself.

Or so you like to think.
So I like to think, yeah. My wife thinks you can't get dumber than me.

Do you ever put your foot down and say, "Ray wouldn't do that!"
Sure. For the first episode of this season ["Fun With Debra"], we had an outline of a story where Debra wanted to have fun with me. In the first outline, Ray embraces the idea of her wanting to golf with him, and I just thought that was totally false. This guy would never want his wife golfing with him. It would make him miserable just thinking about it.

You and Patricia seem to have a great time working together. How do you manage that after all these years?
Me and Patty? We look like we're having fun? [laughs] No, we get along. Not to toot my own dumb horn, but I have a way of getting along with everybody. Every actor's personality is different, and I kinda blend in with it. With Patty, she's easy to get along with, but . . . Let's put it this way, in real life, I don't think she'd ever be dating me.

Are you ever afraid of her when you have to fight on the set?
I don't think she's ever physically hurt me, no. Though in the PMS episode ["Bad Moon Rising"], she threw me into the wall. I've had fights with Brad. That gets a little scary. I've twisted a couple of things during those. I mean, look at him. But Patty, no. Patty I can swat away.

Does Ray have any major issues, or is he just a regular guy?
Well, he's neurotic. We've transferred some of my neuroses to him. He's insecure. I don't know if that's normal. Is that normal? To be neurotic and insecure?

Does your wife Anna give you feedback about the show?
Yes. She watched last night's show, and even though she laughed out loud, which is rare for her, she still came away saying, "But, boy, why are you and Patty married to each other? There's no sweetness anywhere!" I said, "Well, yes there is." But she does have a point. Sometimes we have to remember that a little bit of sweetness goes a long way. I think Debra and Ray were a lot sweeter to each other in the first year. That's how marriage is.

I think the viewers who've watched the show for a long time assume that there's love there.
I guess, but you do have to show it now and again. It's like Archie Bunker saying the most horrible things, and you're thinking that he's the worst person in the world. But then you see that one moment where he's sweet with Edith, and it buys him a few more weeks.

I just saw the episode when you see Robert's date eat a fly.
You know that look that I had when I saw her eat the fly? I had to hold this strained, intense look of disbelief for so long, and the pressure was building up in my head, so that when I finally exploded and said, "She ate it!" I almost fainted! I felt the blood going to my head, and I felt myself losing consciousness. I was ready to yell "Cut!" but I just hoped that it would go away. I did that little dip, and then the blood came back.

Your expression in that scene was so intense! What were you thinking?
I was thinking, "Who is this crazy woman? Did I just see what I saw?" The second time we did it, I was thinking, "Don't faint!" It was a little bit of a departure for us, because it was so bizarre. But I've always said it's okay as long as you react the way you would in real life. If something weird happens, then I just want to see the most incredulous reaction. That keeps it grounded in reality.

What do you think you'll do when the show's over?
Well, my wife thinks I'm gonna be home a lot. Could you tell her that isn't true?

EPISODE 17
THE GAME

PHIL: THIS SHOW IS WHAT THE GREAT GARRY MARSHALL CALLS A "STUCK-IN-A" SHOW. (STUCK IN A CAR, STUCK IN AN ELEVATOR, ETC.) HERE, THE FAMILY IS STUCK IN THE HOUSE WITH NO CABLE TV, SO THEY HAVE TO INTERACT WITH EACH OTHER. THEY PLAY A GAME — A REAL GAME CALLED SCRUPLES. WE LOVED IT, BECAUSE NOT ONLY DOES THAT GAME LET US TALK ABOUT THE PERSONAL, MORAL, AND EMOTIONAL ISSUES THAT WE'VE MADE THE HEART OF THE SHOW, BUT BECAUSE THIS IS THEATER: A TWO-ACT PLAY, FIVE ACTORS, ONE SET, TALKING. THERE'S ENOUGH MTV-STYLE CUTTING AROUND ON TV. THIS IS THE KIND OF SHOW WE GREW UP WITH AND TRIED TO EMULATE: ALL IN THE FAMILY, THE HONEYMOONERS, MARY TYLER MOORE, THE ODD COUPLE. REAL SITUATIONS, REAL PEOPLE — HOPEFULLY REAL FUNNY.

Ray: To me, this was one of our best shows in year one. It was the first of the shows that start with a minimal plot and escalate into a rich, funny half-hour. We've done many shows like this since then, and they are always my favorites.

SEASON 2

EPISODE 33
THE LETTER

PHIL: A BIT OF A MILESTONE EPISODE. THIS BIG SCENE, WHERE DEBRA'S LETTER TO MARIE IS READ ALOUD BY FRANK IN FRONT OF RAY, ROBERT, AND, HORRIFYINGLY, MARIE, IS THE ESSENCE OF WHAT'S GOOD ABOUT THE SHOW: THE CHARACTERS, ALL INVOLVED IN ONE MAIN STORY. (WE DON'T DO SECONDARY, OR "B" STORIES.) THAT MAIN STORY IS DERIVED FROM CHARACTER, SUPPORTS AND EXPLORES CHARACTER, AND ALL THE LAUGHS COME FROM CHARACTER. THE STORY COULD BE DONE AS DRAMA. BUT BECAUSE OF THE TONE OF THE WRITING, AND THE MARVELOUS ENSEMBLE WORK OF THE CAST, WE HOPEFULLY HAVE COMEDY. AND WE THINK THE COMEDY IS RICHER BECAUSE IT KEEPS A FOOT IN REALITY. THAT'S THE ONLY WAY YOU CAN TRULY IDENTIFY WITH IT. FOR EVERY SHOW, WE ASK OURSELVES, "COULD THIS HAPPEN?" THE SAD PART IS, IT USUALLY DID HAPPEN TO ONE OF US.

Ray: Probably one of our top ten episodes. Definitely the best of year two. I shouldn't rate the episodes, since all of them are close to me, but I'm anal and that's what I do.

EPISODE 38
THE CHECKBOOK

Ray: My brother Richard, a real policeman, once told me that his greatest fear was public speaking. He would rather have to face a criminal with a gun than have to speak publicly. With me, of course, it was just the opposite. I could never have the courage to do what he does. So here he is, at the far right, facing his greatest fear on national TV. After the show, I thought it would only be right to return the favor, so I arrested a jaywalker.

PHIL: WE DON'T DO SLAPSTICK VERY OFTEN, BUT WE COULDN'T RESIST THIS TRIBUTE TO SILENT COMEDIES: RAY, BEHIND A WALL OF GLASS IN THE BACKGROUND, FRANTICALLY TRIES TO DEPOSIT MONEY IN THE ATM BEFORE DEBRA REACHES THE TELLER AND DISCOVERS

THAT RAY'S SCREWED UP THE CHECKBOOK. THE BEST PART OF WRITING FOR A SITCOM IS THAT YOU CAN DREAM THIS STUFF UP, A WHOLE SET IS BUILT FOR YOUR STUPID IDEA, ACTORS DO IT, CAMERAS FILM IT, AND THEN IT'S ACTUALLY ON TV. THE COP ON THE RIGHT IS RAY'S REAL BROTHER, WHO ROBERT IS BASED ON. RICHARD IS A HERO, NOT ONLY BECAUSE HE'S A NEW YORK POLICE OFFICER, BUT ALSO BECAUSE OF THE SHOW — HE HAS TO GO THROUGH LIFE WITH PEOPLE THINKING HE IS EXACTLY LIKE ROBERT.

29

AN INTERVIEW WITH PATRICIA HEATON

When your husband is a clueless, over-grown kid and your mother-in-law is a manipulative mastermind, it's tough to keep your cool—which is why Debra gave up on that decades ago. Instead, she fights a pitched battle, openly challenging Ray's selfishness and deceit, or plotting to over-throw Marie and her passive-aggressive tyranny. Debra may inevitably retreat, defeated, but she still clings to the hope that, some day, these utterly unhinged humans she calls "family" might change their evil ways.

They never will change, of course. But don't tell Debra that, because she's funny when she's angry. (Don't tell her that, either.)

Patricia Heaton can relate to Debra's predicament at least a little bit, since she balances her role on the show with the challenges of raising four kids and main-taining a happy marriage. Although there's no way that her real mother-in-law is as taxing as Marie, Patricia seems to have learned a lot from playing Debra, from the importance of accepting the flaws in the person you marry to the triteness of sweater sets.

How was your audition for the show?
When I came in to read for the part, I had to get in and get out really fast because I had a babysitter issue. I think what kind of worked about it was, I needed a job because I hadn't worked for a while. I think I'm very much like Debra: I've got stuff to do, I've got the kids, I don't want to be hassled. I think that's what came across in the reading. Just like a real person: "Let's go! Let's do this! I gotta go!"

What were your first impressions of Ray?
I had never heard of Ray before. So when I saw him . . . he doesn't come across as charismatic right off the bat, to put it diplomatically. So I didn't put much stock in his show. But I knew the writing was really good.

Phil and Ray said that you were the only one to kiss Ray in the audition.
Yeah, when I was called back. I was called a day or two later to see Les Moonves at CBS. I said to Ray, "Do you mind if I kiss you for this?" And he said, "Sure!" I real-ized what a big deal that was. But thank

God I did it. The network thing is very scary most of the time. You have the busi-ness people, and the head of the network, and all these people who can make a deci-sion that will change your life, all in one place. You get one shot at doing it. There are maybe two pages of material.

So you were reading in front of all these people.
You know what? I wasn't really nervous. There's a certain adrenaline pump that starts going. But Ray and I were showing each other pictures of our kids right beforehand. It was very easy—we were just kind of chatting. We were both parents in real life, and we knew what that's like. And I knew that Phil and Michael Lembeck, who was directing the pilot, were really behind me.

Phil said they had looked at hundreds of actresses, and you were clearly the only one who was perfect for the part.
Oh, I never heard that. This is the thing—the writing is so much like real marriage. I don't know how many women who auditioned are actually married with kids. It's still a little unusual. But I totally related to it. It was just like I was talking myself. It wasn't any stretch at all.

Debra is sort of WASPy.
At first I didn't know where she was from or who her parents were. That influences things, like how she dresses. Shoes and stuff are really important—they make you walk a certain way and feel a certain way about yourself. I'm very affected by what I wear, so I needed to know where she was from so I would know how to dress. It was decided pretty quickly that she was from Connecticut, from a slightly different socioeconomic strata than Ray.

My parents, played by Katherine Helmond and Bob Culp, take vacations in Vietnam and they're members of the

Metropolitan Museum and they go to the opera. It's a very different lifestyle. There was an episode where we went to their house in Connecticut for Christmas, and it was filled with all kinds of modern art and sculpture—very sophisticated tastes. That's pretty much where she's from.

You mentioned the way Debra dresses. What do you think her clothes say?
She's been wearing basically the same sweater set and jeans for eight years. So you know for sure that it's about the show and the character, not any kind of fashion thing. We don't have fancy sets, we don't have fancy wardrobe, we just have really great writing. Great, fleshed-out, multi-dimensional characters.

Everyone on the show seems to have a family.
Ray has four kids. Brad has two. Even the writers have two, three, four kids. We all want to get home at a decent hour. I have four children. They're four, six, eight, and ten years old. I was pregnant twice on the show, in real life. They didn't write it in, so they had to go to some lengths to work around my pregnancy.

How did they do that?
It was a certain suspension of disbelief on the part of the audience. Apparently Debra had a lot of Ding-Dongs and Ho-Hos that year, because I gained about fifty pounds. They put me in these great big shirts and they raised the couch up, so that when I walked behind it you couldn't see my belly. And I would carry laundry and always be sitting with a pillow on top of me or something.

You've been playing Debra for so many years now. How has your relationship to her changed?
It's like an old glove that's comfortable and broken in and contoured to your hand. Yet they've given me some, boy . . . we had an episode that aired the week before last ["Thank You Notes"], where Debra tries to get Amy on her side against Marie, and Debra just goes ballistic. To have that kind of stuff going on in the eighth year is great. We haven't gone any place that's unrealistic. Everything that we've been doing has been just layered and layered on through the years so that it's really organic.

What is your favorite year of the show?
Right now, this year! The addition of Monica Horan as Amy has been great. And her family—Chris Elliott and Fred Willard and Georgia Engel. They've added so much. They're hilarious. And the fact that Amy and Robert are married opens up story lines for everybody.

How do you and Ray get along? After countless scenes together, do you ever feel, "I'm ready to divorce this man!"?
I always look forward to scenes with just the two of us. It's the way they write for the two of us. So many people come up to me—it's not just married couples, but gay couples and grandparents, all sorts of people—and say, "Your relationship with Ray is exactly like my relationship with my partner!" One man said to me, just last week, "Sometimes I look at my partner, and I think, 'You're so stupid!'" The show is really about

human relationships. Anytime you make a commitment to somebody, you are bound to run into problems. For better or for worse, that's the vow.

Or for worse and worse and worse!
Yes!

It's better to know that your man is flawed before you marry him, so it doesn't take you by surprise.
Yes, because if you're all in love and it's paradise, you're going to be shocked. You're going to think, "I made a mistake!" But that's what actually happens in a relationship. It's not a mistake.

That's at the heart of the show. The characters constantly give each other a hard time, but underneath it all, there's an unspoken acceptance of each other. That's what family is. You're dealt this hand. You weren't even given a choice about the people you love, you just do it because you've been with them all your life. But that doesn't mean that you like them all the time, either.

It's not contradictory to dislike a family member in some way. It's just part of the package.
It's just the reality of being a human being. On this show, everybody recognizes their own weaknesses. Except for Marie. She's the one person who doesn't see what she's doing. That makes all the difference. That's why she gets away with so much and wins so much of the time.

EPISODE 41
GOOD GIRLS

PHIL: THIS IS LIKE "THE LETTER,"
ANOTHER EXAMPLE OF THE KIND OF
BROADWAY-STYLE COMEDY THAT HAS
DEFINED US. THE SCENE BELOW,
WHERE WE FIND OUT JUST WHO'S
REALLY BEEN A "GOOD GIRL" AND
WHO HAS NOT, HAS REVELATIONS
OF CHARACTER THAT GO OFF LIKE
FIREWORKS. THIS WAS AN EXCITING
NIGHT TO BE AT THE SHOW.

Ray: This is one of my wife's favorite episodes. That's saying a lot, 'cause she usually hates anything I'm in.

THE WEDDING

Ray: I know this is weird, and probably paranoid, but I remember clearly thinking during this scene that I should have brushed my teeth. That's what I remember about the moment. I couldn't relax, thinking, "What if I have bad breath?! Patty is right in the line of fire! Why didn't I brush my damn teeth?! And while I'm at it, my nose hair could probably use a trim." It's not romantic or emotional, but it's the truth.

PHIL: WE DON'T DO "FANTASY" EPISODES ON THE SHOW — IT'S JUST NOT THE STYLE WE WORK IN. BUT WE DO ENJOY THE "FLASHBACK" EPISODES THAT USUALLY END EVERY SEASON. THESE ARE WONDERFUL WAYS TO ILLUMINATE THE BACK STORIES OF THE CHARACTERS AND SHOW THE HIGH POINTS IN THEIR LIVES. I LOOK AT THIS PICTURE AND GET SENTIMENTAL, AS IF IT WERE A REAL WEDDING PHOTO OF PEOPLE I LOVE. IF YOU FEEL THE SAME WAY, MAYBE YOU WATCH TOO MUCH TELEVISION.

ANNA ROMANO AND MONICA HORAN

When your husband discusses your marriage with his blockhead friends who don't understand women, that's tough. When your husband discusses your marriage with a room filled with sitcom-writing blockheads, that's intolerable cruelty. So how do Anna Romano (Ray's wife) and Monica Horan (Phil's wife) deal with seeing their lowest moments dramatized for an entire nation?

Anna and Monica are quick to remind us that we're talking about fictional characters and fictional situations. Comedy is about exaggeration, about taking one small nugget of an idea—an argument you overheard in the grocery store, say—and running with it. True, Ray Barone's childlike demeanor is sometimes a little too realistic for comfort. But Debra? She's an amalgamation of a bunch of impatient, bossy women. She really has very little to do with either Anna or Monica. In fact, both wives say that they're pretty damn good-natured about the whole situation.

But that's obviously just an act, considering how hotheaded and difficult Debra can be.

Do you ever get sick of seeing your personal life on the show?

Anna: It was hard at first, because people really thought that all those stories were about us, that all that stuff happened to us. So I had to say, "No, we're not that crazy!" But it doesn't bother me now. The writers all have a story to tell.

What do you think of Ray's character on the show?

Anna: Sometimes I watch the episodes and I think, "I just want to smack him!" I can't believe how stupid he plays just to get his way. I can relate that to some of the stuff that happens at home. Like when he's looking for something. He'll say, "Where's the camera?" And I'll say, "Did you look anywhere?" "No." "It's in the drawer." "What drawer?" It's like having five children instead of four. I wonder if people think he's annoying. But then again, I'm so close to it, maybe that's why it's annoying to me.

His character personifies the kind of husband who tries to get away with not having to grow up.

Anna: That's how it is at home . . . somewhat. Eighty percent of that. He'll come home from work, and I've just settled everyone down, and he'll come in like, "Come on! I'll give you a punch!" I'll say, "What are you doing? Tone it down. It's nine o'clock, I want them in bed."

How much of the show do you see as coming from your relationship?

Monica: It's all of our lives. So much of it, it's unbelievable. But it's all of us, so there'll be some stories that are closer to others. With us, of course, we always talk about the PMS episode ["Bad Moon Rising"]. That one was a little surreal, because it was literally an entire conversation from our marriage.

And a lot of other people's marriages!

Monica: That's why it works so well—because we're not alone. I remember I told a friend, "You have to watch this PMS episode. This is me and Phil. If you want to know us better, watch this episode." And then, when it aired and I was watching it, I thought, "She's going to think I'm a freak! She's going to think

I'm horrible!" So when I called her, I said, "Are you afraid of me now? Are you afraid of us?" And she said, "No, it's us, too."

It must be strange to have a dramatization of your life history in syndication!

Monica: The PMS episode has been on the air for so long, and all of the writers and Ray and Phil brought so much of their lives to bear in it, that when I see it now, I think, "My God! We do not relate to each other that way anymore." When I saw that episode for the first time, I said to Phil, "You really do hear me!" Because if you look at the show, it's not, "Oh, Debra's a maniac" or "Ray's an idiot." They're just having communication problems.

When I saw it, I thought, "Ray sure is handling this well!"

Monica: That's poetic license. Even if Phil can't say it in the moment, the fact that he can write it shows you what he wants to be saying. And also, therapy helped. That was pretty cool, to be able to look at that and say, "We don't talk like that to each other anymore. We communicate a lot better, and it's not always so fraught."

So you're charting your relationship against Debra and Ray's?

Monica: Exactly! Another episode that was us was "The Can Opener." I literally did cry and say, "I'm not an idiot! I'm not stupid! I can buy a can opener!" It allows you to look at yourself more objectively.

EPISODE 59
THE TOASTER

Ray: This episode has one of Frank Barone's top ten lines of all time. (I really like rating things.) Doris says, "I'm not some trophy wife," and Frank replies, "Trophy wife? What contest in Hell did I win?" This show also marked my real brother Rich's second appearance, as a security guard.

PHIL: PEOPLE ALWAYS ASK ME, "WHAT DO YOUR PARENTS THINK OF THEIR PORTRAYALS ON THE SHOW?" WELL, I WATCHED THIS EPISODE WHILE SITTING NEXT TO THEM ON THE COUCH. AND THIS SHOW HAPPENED TO COME DIRECTLY FROM SOMETHING THEY ACTUALLY DID (SEE "REAL-LIFE MOTHERS" ON PAGE 74). THERE'S A MOMENT IN THE SHOW WHERE RAYMOND CALLS HIS PARENTS "YOU PSYCHOPATHS." MY MOTHER LAUGHED, ELBOWED MY FATHER, AND SAID, "HEY, WE'RE THE PSYCHOPATHS!" IT'S NICE WHEN YOU CAN MAKE YOUR PARENTS PROUD OF YOUR WORK.

EPISODE 62
ROBERT'S DATE

PHIL: ONE OF OUR MOST POPULAR EPISODES. ROBERT STARTS HANGING OUT WITH HIS BLACK PARTNER, JUDY, AND BEGINS TO CHANGE HIS STYLE, FRIGHTENING HIS FAMILY. ROBERT BECOMES SO "SUPERFLY" THAT AT ONE POINT RAY MUST TELL HIM, "WE'RE ITALIAN, ROBERT. 'WHACK' MEANS SOMETHING ELSE TO US."

Ray: Funny clothes, funny dancing — what more do you need?

AN INTERVIEW WITH BRAD GARRETT

handful of shows that didn't make it. But I started as a stand-up, and I was doing stand-up for about twenty years before I got *Raymond*. Believe it or not, I started stand-up when I was sixteen. I looked thirty, and I was able to get into all the clubs. My main living for all those years was stand-up.

What were your early jokes about?
When you're sixteen, you joke about being grounded. You know: "Take my nanny, please!" A lot of the material was about my height, because I was six feet at thirteen—kind of a giant.

And did you enjoy doing stand-up from the beginning?
Loved it, loved it! It's something that finds you. I couldn't *not* do it. Once in a while, someone will come up to me and go, "I'm thirty-five, I really want to get onstage as a comic, and I don't know how to do it." And right away, you know that these people aren't destined to do it, because—and Ray knows this—you play anywhere. You cannot *help* but get up. It's a type of craft that just eats away at you. It's something that you don't learn and you can't teach. You're either born a comic or you're not. It's the way you perceive life, it's how you tell a story, it's something that just makes you want to express yourself in a funny way. And gosh knows you can't learn timing. You have it or you don't.

Being overshadowed by your own brother is never easy, particularly when he's a foot shorter than you. Robert Barone has suffered the fate of the prodigal son his entire life—without the part where he gets to squander his inheritance on wine and women. It's the classic story: Every time Robert does something good, Ray comes in and makes him look bad. Every time Robert gets a break, Ray gets an even bigger break. Every time Robert finds the girl of his dreams, Ray catches her snacking on dead flies.

Like a true gentleman, though, Robert takes it all in stride—when he's not whining and stomping his feet and shouting,

"No fair!" Will Robert's marriage to Amy bring an end to Ray's status as the favorite son? Brad Garrett's answer to that is: Fat chance. Still, despite the downtrodden role he helped to create, he's found great joy in playing "the gloomy brother." With an attitude that's far more optimistic than something we might hear out of Robert's mouth, Brad talks about the incredible luck of being on a hit show, and why it's not over until the tall guy wears a sombrero.

You did stand-up before *Everybody Loves Raymond*?
This wasn't my first TV job—I did a

When did you start to focus on TV?
My first real TV job was a pilot for CBS

in '88 or so, *First Impressions*. I was twenty-six, and I played the single father of a little girl who looked nothing like me. They made me from Nebraska, lightened my hair, and put me in a plaid shirt and penny loafers. These guys were like, "We'll take a seven-foot Jew and make him from Nebraska." It went four episodes. My TV job right before *Raymond* was called *The Pursuit of Happiness*, which was done by the people who did *Frasier*. I played a gay lawyer—I love to do things against my type. I mean, I'm big, I'm ethnic. This was before *Will & Grace* and before *The Ellen Show*. The writers' and producers' thing wasn't to get me to play a really over-the-top gay guy. He was just a regular guy who was coming out of the closet in his forties. I loved the writing. Then this little show called *Third Rock from the Sun* went against us, and we were history.

Did you take any acting classes?
I've always studied. I was at the Lee Strasberg Theatre Institute when I was eighteen. I've always worked on acting to help with dramas. But sitcom stuff is all timing. I don't think it's something you can learn in a class.

What did you bring to the table in forming Robert's character?
This is a character I knew. I went in with this character. They were supposedly looking for a Danny DeVito type, a little bulldog nipping at Ray's heels. They wanted a real scrappy type of guy to play Ray's brother. They didn't expect this big, towering guy. But when I read the pilot, I knew the writing was very, very unique. My managers said, "You're up for three other pilots with big-name

people in them. What are you doing?" And I said, "This guy can write. I want to go for this one." They're saying, "But no one knows this guy." The rest is history, as they say.

A good choice!
I got lucky! It's all about the writing. And I just knew the character. Out of the gate, I said, "Instead of a scrappy, excitable type of guy, wouldn't it be funny to play him as someone who was so beaten, so downtrodden?" What I use for Robert is, in the back of his mind he's thinking, "Raymond is an only child, they just forgot to tell me." He's a guy who's used to coming in second. He's resigned to that fact.

But he gets these glimmers of hope.
Which is what keeps everybody going. They're glimmers, but he doesn't always know they're glimmers. Sometimes he knows. Sometimes he says, "Boy, this may be my way out." And what he's learning, at any rate, is that he'll never be Raymond, and that there are parts of Raymond he really doesn't want to be. We are who we are.

You've really been at the center of the show lately.
I think Robert is one of the last characters to be fully fleshed out. Up until last season, Robert wasn't married, didn't have this, didn't have that. I had four lines in the pilot. I've kind of been a character who would say a few things and disappear for twenty minutes. But more and more, they're bringing in Robert's life. As far as family dynamics go, he's really going to be one of the last characters to go through everything.

What do you think makes the show so special?
It's like life. People talk, people listen. This is one of the few comedies where there are shots of people listening. You rarely have that in comedy. On this show, it's about the moments. Because that's where life lives, in those tiny, tiny things. Like around the table in the "Misery Loves Company" episode. We all know that couple who's been married for three months and are experts on marriage. We all know older people who are resigned to it, or who are just hanging on. And we know the couples like Ray and Debra, who live it every day way past the honeymoon. The writers have an amazing way with family dynamics. Just about every episode is about life and family. I mean, if I ever walk in wearing a sombrero, it's over.

How do you think you'll remember the experience of being on *Everybody Loves Raymond*?
Careerwise, it's probably the greatest time of my life. I think what makes this cast such a good group is that there isn't one person here who takes it for granted. To get on a hit is a one-in-a-million shot, but to get on a hit that you're proud of, a critical hit, a show that you know in twenty years will stand up, that's a blessing. I was watching *All in the Family* the other night, and it's still amazing. The "Misery Loves Company" episode of our show had a real heartfelt feeling. When it ended, when we looked at each other and we all toasted each other, you could believe that we were a family. A lot of times we go for the joke, and a lot of times we don't. But we're able to tackle issues on a human level, and I think that is what makes the show a classic.

EPISODE 65
RAY HOME ALONE

Ray: We always try to police ourselves with reality. But let's be honest, if we were being real, a show called "Ray Home Alone" would be thirty minutes of me running around in my underwear, singing songs, and eating peanut butter.

EPISODE 71
DANCING WITH DEBRA

PHIL: HERE WE DID AN EXTENDED, NO-DIALOGUE DANCE SEQUENCE
SET TO LOUIS PRIMA'S "SING, SING, SING," PLAYED LIVE BY A BIG
BAND, AND TRIED TO MOVE THE STORY FORWARD AT THE SAME
TIME — JUST LIKE A MUSICAL. I'M ALWAYS TRYING TO GET MUSIC
AND DANCING INTO THE SHOW, NOT JUST BECAUSE OF MY STRONG,
YET HETEROSEXUAL ATTRACTION TO THE FORM, BUT BECAUSE WE
TRULY BELIEVE THAT NOTHING BEATS FUNNY DANCING.

EPISODE 72
ROBERT MOVES BACK?

PHIL: THE CROTCH IN ROBERT'S PANTS COULDN'T POSSIBLY BE THAT LOW FOR AMY TO FIT INTO THEM THE WAY SHE DOES. BUT ONCE IN A GREAT WHILE, REALITY, LIKE ROBERT'S PANTS' CROTCH, MUST BE STRETCHED JUST ENOUGH FOR THE LAUGH. WE HAD THE HONOR OF MEETING TIM CONWAY RECENTLY, AT THE CBS SEVENTY-FIFTH ANNIVERSARY SHOW, AND HE TOLD US THIS BIT WAS "THE FUNNIEST SIGHT GAG ON TV IN YEARS." WE CAN NOW DIE HAPPY.

RICHARD AND ROBERT ROMANO

Brothers are either best friends, ruthless competitors, or sworn enemies, depending on what day it is. When they have your back, you can't lose. When they're mad at you, you can't win. But Ray Romano can't stand to have anyone mad at him, so his brothers Richard (*middle*) and Robert (*right*) had his back more often than not.

And how does he thank them? By creating an envious, mopey character out of Richard's life and giving him Robert's name. Despite such abuse, both brothers seem anxious to shed light on the many reasons why Robert . . . well, you know.

RICHARD ROMANO

You coined the phrase "Everybody loves Raymond"?
It was a running conversation at the dinner table. Raymond was always the life of the party, with his quick wit and his stories and his jokes. And my mother, being the mom that she is, would always look at me and see me being left out of the conversation, and she'd say, "Richard, so . . . tell us about your work." And you can't really relate that many NYPD stories that are entertaining. Ray and I, we're only eighteen months apart, and we've always had a very fierce competition, but a good-natured one. So I looked at Raymond and I said, "You want to hear my stories? I'll tell you the difference between me and the stories you just heard from Raymond. Raymond goes to work and he tells jokes, and

people laugh, and they all love him. But I go to work, and I get shot at, stabbed at, spit on, cursed at. Everybody hates me. Everybody loves Raymond."

How do you feel about having a character based on you?
It's great. But when I was a cop, the other cops were ruthless about it. There was an episode where the parents thought Robert was gay. I really got the business that day. They were always kidding me. One time, we were on a stakeout, and I was lying on the floor of a housing project. It was cold and there were bugs—it was gross. All of a sudden, my partner started laughing and couldn't stop. I said, "What are you laughing about? Shut up, you're gonna give us away!" And he said, "Sarge, it's just so ironic that you're here in this, and your brother's doing backflips in his swimming pool in Hollywood." That's the way it went. But anybody who knows me knows that there are a lot of differences between me and the character.

How was your relationship with Ray when you were younger?
He was like my best friend growing up. We were very competitive in any sport, you name it. We used to wrestle each other. We had a crazy household. It was a lot of fun. The only thing we didn't have a rivalry over was girls. We never liked the same girl growing up.

Did you two fight?
We used to share a room. One night, when I was ten and he was maybe eight, we had a spitball fight. We're in our bedroom and we hear our father saying, "Shuddup!" We finally had to stop, but before we did, he spit on me! So he fell asleep, and I went into the bathroom and got a cup of water, and I poured it over his head to wake him up. He was really mad!

You couldn't hold back from one-upping each other.
Absolutely. Just like the show. That part of the show is true.

ROBERT ROMANO

Your name is Robert, but that character is really based on Richard?
Using my name was Ray's way of throwing me a bone. But whenever anyone says to him, "Why isn't your other brother on the show?" Ray always says, "Because he's too normal." I always laugh and say, "Well, if I'm normal, then define normal."

What was it like to have Ray as a big brother?
Growing up with Ray was wonderful. Ray was always very good to us. He never wanted to be confrontational, he never wanted to cause any bad blood. He and I had to share a really tiny room with bunk beds, and he was always entertaining. He was always playing for me, whether it was fighting with our accordion door or doing something else to make me laugh. It was really exciting for me when he first started out in comedy. I would go everywhere with him. I was thrilled, even at three in the morning when he was playing Pips Comedy Club to an audience of two, including the drunk emcee.

Was he the best comedian at the clubs?
It was more *who* he is; he's such a likable guy. He's not intimidating, he's not threatening. It's his personality that makes him stand out. I mean, he's been doing the same material for the last five years! Because he's so relatable, it makes a difference. He's just a great storyteller.

Everyone says he's a real perfectionist.
Yes, he is, if by perfectionist you mean anal-retentive and neurotic.

EPISODE 74
BOOB JOB

PHIL: A WEEK OR SO BEFORE WE CAME BACK TO BEGIN OUR FOURTH SEASON, THE EMMY NOMINATIONS WERE ANNOUNCED. WE HAD NOT RECEIVED A SINGLE NOMINATION IN OUR FIRST THREE YEARS. BUT THIS SEASON, THE ENTIRE CAST HAD BEEN NOMINATED — EXCEPT FOR BRAD. SO, BEFORE OUR FIRST TABLE READ, I SAID A FEW WORDS ABOUT HOW EXCITING IT WAS TO GET ALL THESE NOMINATIONS, AND I MADE A POINT OF SAYING THAT EVERYONE GOT EXACTLY WHAT THEY DESERVED. YOU CAN SEE BRAD'S FACE HERE AS I'M SAYING THAT. YOU CAN ALSO SEE A MAN WALKING UP BEHIND HIM. THAT'S BOB BARKER, WHO PROCEEDED TO PRESENT BRAD WITH A "BEST ACTOR IN THE WORLD" AWARD FROM US.

Ray: This is the difference between Phil and me. This was a show about "boobs," and all he remembers is Bob Barker.

AN INTERVIEW WITH PETER BOYLE

It takes a strong man to stand by a strong woman. Frank Barone would prefer to sit. Whether he's hurling insults at his nutty wife, espousing a man's basic right to do next to nothing, or shoving a salty snack into his mouth, Frank is an enigma. What does he really believe in? Whose side is he on? What's that he just spilled all over the floor, and why is he kicking it under the rug?

When you're married to a complicated, demanding woman, sometimes it pays to keep things simple, to lie low, to keep your trap shut. Other times, it pays to whine loudly, at least until someone fixes you a hot meal. For all of his unpre-dictable outbursts and bizarre antics, Frank knows how to get what he wants. And for some sick reason, we want him to get it, too.

While Peter Boyle is sweet, thoughtful, and smart—in other words, the exact opposite of Frank—his enthusiasm for Frank's unhinged behavior comes through clearly on-screen, and that may be a big part of why we root for Frank even in his most absurdly selfish moments.

How did you learn comedy?
First of all, it was growing up in the family I grew up in. My dad was a very funny guy, and we had a lot of laughs. Then, when I was studying acting, I got into improv. I worked at the Premise and at Second City in Chicago. And I went on tour with a road company of Neil Simon's *The Odd Couple.* So I became aware of certain rules of comedy—you've got to hear the punch line, and you've got to set it up a certain way. Since we do this show with a live audience, you're always learning and sensing the audience listening and going with the joke. As important as character is, it's also the timing.

When did you start to move from movies to TV?
Since the late '80s, I'd done a series of guest shots. The first was on *Cagney & Lacey,* and then on a show called *Midnight Caller.* I also did a show in the late '80s called *Joe Bash* that was on the air for six episodes. It was an interesting show about two cops on the beat, by the guy who created *Barney Miller.* It was basically a

half-hour comedy, but it was filmed with one camera and no audience. It's really hard to do comedy when there's nobody there to laugh. Now, looking back, I've realized how crazy hard that was.

Tell me about your audition for *Everybody Loves Raymond.*
I was auditioning for a bunch of pilots, and got a script for *Raymond.* And I did something that I've never done: I went to the audition with my wife and two daughters and a friend. We had trouble getting on the lot at Universal, and then we had trouble finding a parking space. Then we had trouble finding the spot where the audition was happening. So when I arrived, I was angry. I scared Phil and Ray. But they liked it. It fit the character. Then we did the pilot, and they had a good director, and then after the director directed, Phil Rosenthal came in and really directed. The pilot was really good. That I knew. It had an original sound to it and it was funny and the parents were odd and quirky and not typical. At that point, sitcoms were all like two bachelors with two kids. I'm very grateful to my wife and daughters for coming with me to the audition—they brought me great good fortune!

How was it to do TV after so many years in the movies?
It's easy in one way, and it's real hard in another. A sitcom has its own rules, which I had to learn fast. Since we shoot it in front of a live audience and with four

cameras, it's not like a movie. You can't stop and start. You don't do a couple of lines and then stop. You have to do a whole scene. It can be ten pages, and you have to know them. If you don't know them, the writers, who are all standing there, don't laugh. If you do it right, they laugh. They're their lines.

How much time do you have to learn your lines?
Two or three days. It's not that it's that hard. It's that I have a tendency to paraphrase, and you can't do that.

Because it changes the joke.
Exactly! There are the rules of comedy and the rhythm that they write in. I had to learn to adjust to that. I would rehearse a lot; the very first year, Ray and I lived in the same apartment complex, a temporary apartment. His family was back in New York. We would rehearse on the weekends. Ray is one of the hardest-working people in the world.

When the show stuck around, did you think, "Hey, when will I get to do movies again?"
I've got what they call a nut. I've got expenses. I had a family, my daughters were in school in New York. So this was steady, and it was a good thing. The movie business isn't steady. So it was a no-brainer.

It's been a long job.
But it's been creative, and it's as pleasant as it can be. We're all very different. Somehow we get along.

No one is just setting up someone else's jokes.

Exactly. The characters and the writing are everything. The play's the thing. That's one of the great things about this show. The hardest parts and the best parts of the job are frequently different ends of the same situation. The hardest part is doing all your lines properly. The best part is getting it right and feeling the audience, getting a laugh, feeling the interplay. It's just a lot of fun.

It seems like everyone's having fun. Viewers can tell that.
It's like a team where everybody gets the ball and gets to score a point. Everybody gets to score.

What's your favorite episode?
There's not one clear favorite, but I like the one where Frank and Marie backed the car through the living room ["Wallpaper"]. We enjoyed that. One of the hardest ones was the one where I repaired the stairs and fell through them ["Frank Goes Downstairs"]. That was dangerous stunt work.

How would you describe your character on the show?
He's a curmudgeon. He tends to be kind of eccentric and say anything that pops into his head, regardless of the effect on anybody.

Is Frank ever sweet?
Yes, he has the capacity for tenderness. Not a huge capacity for tenderness, but he's not a bad guy.

What was his most tender moment on the show?
I don't want to mention it.

Why not?

It was too tender. You're liable to think I'm weak!

You don't want Frank to get a wimpy reputation?
Exactly! I was very tender with Marie in one episode. I hugged her, and she had cold cream on her face and I wiped it off. It was very sweet.

How do you get into character?
It's pretty comfortable, like an old jacket or shirt. That's why it's fun being an actor—we get to do this and we get paid for it. That part of it is fun: the part between "Action!" and "Cut!"

I loved last night's episode ["The Contractor"], where Ray is in bed with back pain and you say, "Look at my little crippled boy!"
I loved that line. The great thing about doing a sitcom is, it's really for laughs. It ends in a laugh, rather than in a shootout.

It's great when Frank gets weird.
I love that, too! He is genuinely an odd guy. The other members of the family are a little more accessible, they're a little more identifiable, they're a little more understandable. Frank has an edge.

How do you make those turns from gruffness to cleverness?
I change pitch is what I do. It's the old switcheroo. The old mislead.

Like in that scene where . . .
You remember these scenes better than I do! You've got me at a disadvantage, because I'm trying to remember the scene I just rehearsed!

EPISODE 75
THE CAN OPENER

PHIL: THIS STORY WAS BASED IN FACT, TOO. I CAME HOME ONE NIGHT, AND THERE REALLY WASN'T ANYTHING FOR DINNER. NOTHING WRONG WITH THAT, I THOUGHT, I'LL JUST HAVE A TUNA FISH SANDWICH. I LIKE TUNA FISH. MY WIFE HAD BOUGHT A NEW CAN OPENER, THOUGH — THE KIND THAT REMOVES THE ENTIRE TOP OF THE CAN. WELL, WITHIN A MINUTE, I WAS COVERED IN TUNA JUICE, AND WE HAD A LITTLE FIGHT, WHICH MAY HAVE BEEN FUELED BY ME HAVING TO FEND FOR MYSELF AFTER A LONG DAY AT WORK, AND MY WIFE'S RESENTMENT AT THE INFERENCE THAT SHE SHOULD HAVE DINNER WAITING FOR ME AFTER A LONG DAY WITH THE KIDS. WE DIDN'T COME DOWN ON ONE SIDE OR THE OTHER IN THIS EPISODE, BUT I'D LIKE TO SAY RIGHT HERE THAT SHE WAS RIGHT.

Ray: This is one of my favorite pictures in the book. I look at this picture sometimes and try to duplicate that jump, and I can't do it. There is no way I can get that high. I don't know how I did it. I guess adrenaline and stupidity are a powerful combination. And yet even with that jump, I'm still only eye-to-eye with Brad.

You Bet

Ray: Before each scene, Peter and I always perform a prayer ritual to the comedy gods.

EPISODE 83
LEFT BACK

PHIL: WE DON'T USE THE KIDS THAT MUCH. THERE ARE A COUPLE OF REASONS FOR THAT. ONE, WE WANTED THE SHOW TO BE ABOUT PEOPLE WHO HAVE KIDS, NOT ABOUT KIDS. BESIDES, WE FELT THAT MOST SITCOMS WITH KIDS RELY TOO MUCH ON TODDLERS SPOUTING IMPOSSIBLY PROFESSIONALLY WRITTEN JOKES. AND TWO, IF WE DON'T SHOW THE CHILDREN TOO OFTEN, THEN, WHEN YOU DO SEE THEM, YOU REALLY ENJOY SEEING THEM. AND WE GOT LUCKY, BECAUSE THE SWEETEN KIDS, ALL REAL-LIFE SIBLINGS, ARE WONDERFUL, GENUINE ACTORS, WITHOUT THE CUTESINESS THAT CAN BE A PLAGUE ON THE LAND. AND RAY'S GREAT WITH THEM.

EPISODE 97
ROBERT'S DIVORCE

Ray: Phil is in the kitchen pretending he is me for the gag reel. I was pretending I was him at the time. You can't see it, but I'm off-camera yelling about what a bad actor Phil is.

EPISODE 85
WHAT'S WITH ROBERT?

PHIL: IS ROBERT GAY? THE FAMILY WONDERS ABOUT HIM WHEN HE KEEPS STRIKING OUT WITH WOMEN. MY PARENTS WONDERED ABOUT ME, TOO, WHEN I WAS IN MY TWENTIES AND NOT HAVING MUCH LUCK WITH THE LADIES. I REMEMBER WHAT MY FATHER DID WHEN MY MOTHER TRIED TO BROACH THE SUBJECT WITH ME IN THEIR KITCHEN: HE HELD A CARTON OF MILK TO HIS HEAD.

THE CHRISTMAS PICTURE

Ray: Look how intense Phil gets when he gives notes. What you can't see is that Brad and I are sleeping.

EPISODE 94
SOMEONE'S CRANKY

PHIL: BY THE TIME THE NIGHT OF FILMING COMES AROUND, WE'VE SPENT MANY HOURS POLISHING EVERY DETAIL OF AN EPISODE. ABOUT A WEEK LATER, I SIT IN THE EDITING ROOM AND SEE WHAT WE'VE CAPTURED ON FILM. WITH THE EDITING BAY IN THE BACK OF MY HEAD, I TRY TO MAKE SURE WE DON'T MISS ANYTHING ON SHOW NIGHT. SINCE IT'S IN FRONT OF A LIVE AUDIENCE, YOU REALLY WANT TO GET IT RIGHT ON THE FIRST TAKE. THIS EPISODE CONTAINED A VERY CHALLENGING SCENE WITH BRAD AND PATTY, AND IT WAS GOING TO BE THE FIRST TIME IN OVER NINETY SHOWS THAT I WOULDN'T BE THERE. MY GRANDMOTHER HAD DIED, AND I FLEW TO NEW YORK ON SHOOT NIGHT. I DID, HOWEVER, CALL THE STAGE JUST BEFORE THIS BIG SCENE, AND THEY HELD THE PHONE UP FOR ME TO LISTEN IN. AFTER THE FIRST TAKE, BRAD CAME TO THE PHONE, WE TALKED ABOUT THE SCENE, MADE SOME ADJUSTMENTS, AND HE DID ANOTHER TAKE WHILE I LISTENED. IT TURNED OUT FINE, AND WHAT I LEARNED IS, MAYBE I DON'T NEED TO BE THERE.

Ray: I don't know what this scene was about, because it was the first one in about eighty episodes that I wasn't in. So I went to my dressing room, made a phone call, and used the bathroom. I heard the scene went well.

THE WRITERS' ROOM

The writers' room is ground zero for every episode of the show. Sure, it looks just like an ordinary conference room, with its long table flanked by ergonomic chairs and its wall-to-wall whiteboards. But look a little closer and you'll find strange little details that hint at the darkness and chaos that go on behind closed doors: A Mr. Potato Head. A sports trivia game. A bar of dark chocolate. About twenty small bottles of hot sauce.

This is clearly the stomping ground of strange, unpredictable humans. Indeed, the writers call this room everything from a confessional to a therapist's office. That may sound a little bit intimate for a place of business, but when you start to hear the stories behind the show, you understand why. Audiences relate to the Barones because the writers courageously dredge up their most embarrassing or difficult moments to share in the writers' room— at which point, the other writers snicker and jeer at them. No wonder they need the chocolate and the toys.

The writers took time out from ruth-

lessly mocking each other to describe the pros and cons of squabbling, the parable of the unpacked suitcase, and why marriage means never letting down your guard.

Cast of characters: Tom Caltabiano, Leslie Caveny, Tucker Cawley, Ray Romano, Phil Rosenthal, Mike Royce, Lew Schneider, Mike Scully, Aaron Shure, Steve Skrovan, and Jeremy Stevens.

Most sitcoms these days have multiple story lines. Is it harder to write just one story line per show?
Jeremy: I think it's easier. As it is, this medium is a telescoping of the story. It's twenty-two minutes to start with, so why would you want to telescope stories even more, if the stories are going to have any substance? You're always going to tell a better story if you have more time and you can create great twists. You're able to go obliquely into something and get more surprises.

Mike Scully: I get really frustrated with shows where there are four or five story

lines in twenty-two minutes. They're so choppy; sometimes scenes feel like nothing more than somebody pouring a cup of coffee and then a music cue to the next scene. You don't really get into the characters' feelings, because you're just trying to service the beats of all the stories.

Jeremy: *Scenus Interruptus.* It's like getting just an appetizer at a restaurant. "Hello! Here's the shrimp cocktail. Goodbye." "Wait a minute. Where's the steak?"

What makes an episode work?
Tucker: I think our best shows are the ones that strike a chord, so people say, "I've had that argument" or "My parents have had that fight." My wife and I went away for the weekend and we came home, and I brought our suitcase up to our bedroom and just put it next to our bed. Then, a day or two later, the suitcase was still there, and I thought, "That's weird. Aileen hasn't gotten to that yet. Huh." And I forgot about it. Then, a couple of days later, I noticed it was still there, and now I'm wondering, "What's going on? Why hasn't she put it away?" Then I stubbed my toe on it, and I said, kind of pointedly, "Huh, that suitcase is still there." And she was reading and she just looked up and said, "Yeah, I guess it is." And that's when I knew that it wasn't just procrastination, that Aileen was waiting for me to do it. And at that moment, if I had been a good husband, I would've maybe put it away, or talked to her about it. . . .

Lew: But instead you swore a blood oath.

Tucker: I swore a blood oath to myself silently that I was *not* moving that suitcase. This wasn't even a fight. It was just a stubborn kind of standoff that all couples have. So I pitched this as a story idea to the other writers, and everyone really kind of hooked into it and had examples of their own, and so we developed a story from there.

Tom: When Tucker told us, "I wasn't gonna move that bag," I was shocked. Because I haven't been married and in that mental tug-of-war that goes on. I said, "Tucker, move the bag. This is crazy. Just pick up the bag and move it." And all the married men were like, "Don't move that bag! Do not touch that bag!"

Phil: You have to see that episode ["Baggage"]. Tucker won an Emmy for that one. How, in seven years, did we not think of that fight and what a great metaphor that is? First of all, it's literally baggage. Second, who's going to help the other person? It brought something new to the show, to the relationship with Ray and Debra.

Ray: It was another way to argue.

Phil: Yes, but these stories are few and far between now, these kind of "Oh, we didn't turn over that rock, there's something there!"

Tucker: The night we shot the episode, audience members came down to the railing and started telling me their suitcase stories. "There was a ballpoint pen that was up against the wall, and I wasn't moving it because it was my husband's, and he wasn't moving it because he thought it was my job, and it was there for seven months." I knew right then that we had something good.

It's interesting how people relate to certain episodes.
Jeremy: Two weeks ago, a friend of mine asked me, "Was I indiscreet? Did I talk about what Joan said about her mother?" I said, "What?" and he said, "The show two nights ago, the whole thing that she was talking about with her mother. I don't remember telling you that." He was in trouble with his wife. I told him, "You never did." He said, "It was word for word what's going on in our marriage about her mother."

Mike Scully: It's cool when people are relating to it that much. With the episode where they went to Italy, I was just a fan of the show then, I wasn't working on it. But my wife and I had literally had the same conversation as Ray and Debra, where Debra wanted to go and see other cultures, and Ray said, "I've never really been interested in other cultures." Verbatim, I had said that to my wife a year earlier, and I couldn't believe I was hearing Ray say it. I was watching the show with my wife, and I said, "See, it's not just me! Ray feels the same way." Yes, I know it's pathetic to use sitcom characters to back up your position, but sometimes it's all you've got.

It comes from being honest about your limitations. It always strikes me when I see that episode: "God, if only I could just say that I'm not interested in other cultures!"
Jeremy: The writers' room is a confessional. There's a trust there, because everybody gets ripped apart. It's a confessional in which the priest laughs at you and makes fun of you and mocks you. But you get everything out, and you talk about what's going on with yourself, and with your family. You gotta be willing to be honest.

Mike Scully: The level of openness in the room about people's personal lives is kind of shocking. My wife and I are fairly private people, so to hear everybody talk so comfortably and honestly about what goes on in their families, it takes awhile to get used to. I think that's probably why the first episode I wrote never happened in my life. The next one that I'm writing is something that happened in my real life, but not between me and my wife, it was between me and one of my neighbors. So I'm ready now to betray a neighbor, but not my wife yet.

Jeremy: As soon as you're desperate enough, you'll tell us.

Many of you have been here from the show's start. How have your interactions changed over such a long period?

Steve: There are generations of us. Jeremy, who had a couple of teenagers, and another writer, who also had a couple of teenagers, were constantly being called out of the room during the day to put out teenage fires. And the rest of us with younger kids would roll our eyes. Now I've got a teenager, and it's just a mess. Back then, the older your kids were, the stupider you were. The parents with teenagers didn't know what they were doing. I was sort of in the middle, with kids in the double digits, but not quite teenagers. I was a little smarter than they were, but not much. And people with really little kids were pretty smart, because they knew exactly what needed to be done and what kind of a parent you needed to be. And the absolute smartest people were the people who didn't have kids at all! They knew exactly what you need to do for everything. You just get stupider as you get older, that's what we found.

Tom: For me, being single has become a big part of how I'm perceived by the other writers, because my world is completely different from theirs. Even if it's the most minor thing. Here's a story: There was a big event coming up here in L.A. I was away visiting my father, and Phil was like, "Who are you bringing to this event?" I wasn't going out with anybody, but I had met a very nice person, and I said, "I'm probably going to bring Jessica." So I was away in New Jersey for a week, and when I walk back into the writers' room, it's, "How's your father?" "Great." "Uh, you know, Tom, if you bring that young girl to the event, do you realize the problems that will cause with our wives?" She was very young. . . .

Mike Royce: How young, now?

Tom: She was younger than I thought, let's put it that way. I thought she was maybe twenty-three or twenty-four. Okay, she was a few years younger than that, even. I thought Phil was kidding about not bringing her. But he said, "No, seriously, you should really think about it." What ensued was an hour-long debate, where everybody was projecting their stuff onto me about bringing this girl. The female writers had their own take on it, and there were a few people who didn't say a word the whole time. So I brought this girl to the event, and then, three days later, Tucker says, "Tom, I'm sitting in my living room watching TV, and Aileen walks in and goes, 'What do you think Tom talks to that girl about?' and I said, 'Uh, I don't know.'" His argument with his wife became Debra and Ray's fight in the "Young Girl" episode, which I wrote with Aaron Shure. Robert shows up with a young woman; Frank is proud; and Debra, in public, is like, "Hey, good for him. He can date whoever he wants." Then, later that night, Ray is in the bedroom and Debra walks in and asks, "What could he possibly have in common with that girl?" Ray's like, "I don't know, maybe they don't have to talk."

Mike Royce: My wife knows Tom and likes him. I told her that he was bringing a young woman to the event, and it didn't bother her. But when we went, we walked by you two and she just turned to me and said, "He is such an asshole!"

Tom: Perfect. That's the kind of passion that makes a great story.

It sounds like most of the stories are pulled directly from your lives.
Steve: You get into an argument with your wife, and you realize that this is a bad argument, but it might be a story idea, so you keep it going to see if you can get a second act.

You hope she does something manipulative?

Steve: Yeah, so I can have an act break. Most recently . . . my son is a teenager, and he was having a lot of problems with school. He wasn't going to school for days at a time. We just couldn't get him out of bed. He's too big to pick up and carry anymore. So I wanted to do a story about that, about how that affects your relationship with your wife, and about the different strategies you use to try to get kids to go to school. Then I told a story about how I wet my pants on the Little League field when I was ten years old, in front of everybody. So two of my stories were put together in this one episode ["Home From School"]. Then Phil came in and said there was something that wasn't satisfying about it. And in the meantime, I'd had a huge fight with my son about not going to school, and I had said to him, "You're gonna have to spend the day with me now." And that's what we did. At first it was very contentious—I had to literally drag him out of bed and walk him down the hall. I said, "First you're gonna take a shower, and then you're gonna have breakfast, and if you think going to school is bad, wait until you spend the time with me." But in the course of doing these things, we started talking, and he started talking about his problems, and we had one of the best days of our lives as a father and son because of having to work this out. So we brought that to the story, and Ray did an amazing job with it. We can have something happen in our lives, and writing can do what it was meant to do—help you process it and turn it into a creative thing, and other people can share that and laugh at it, and you can laugh at it, too.

That sounds pretty ideal.
Mike Royce: Most of my stories originated with arguments between me and my wife.

Tom: And my stories are also from fights between me and Mike's wife.

Mike Royce: I have a constant issue with my wife. She's an architect and also a designer. I don't have any say about what's going on designwise in our house, and I shouldn't, but I think she always rides over my opinion when it comes to that. So that makes me want to have an opinion even more, even when I didn't *want* to have an opinion before. That's what the "Tissues" episode is about. Debra takes care of things and Ray demands more say, and then he goes out and gets all these groceries, including these tissues, and the tissues cause the house to catch on fire.

Tom: Great stunt. The crew's eyebrows are just starting to grow back.

Mike Royce: It's like life imitating art imitating life—it just keeps going around and around. She now uses the episode against me in arguments. We have an argument about this kind of thing, and she goes, "This is the whole 'Tissues' thing that you have with me." It's like a reference in our life now. It's become shorthand for some of the core issues of our marriage.

Lew: We always talk about this: When we have fights, our wives say, "This is not a good story" or "Don't make this a story. Don't!" But then sometimes my wife has tried to cheer me up with it. We went skiing with our kids, and we were up at the lodge, and I was coming back from the hot tub carrying my clothes, including my

pants with all my stuff in the pockets. As I got in the elevator, my pants fell, and I dropped the van keys down the space between the floor and the elevator shaft. If you tried a hundred times, you couldn't throw them down there. So now I'm up there and my skis are locked in the car. Nobody can ski, and snowboarders are trying to get on the elevator, and I'm saying, "No, uh, no. You can't use this elevator." I'm holding the door, I'm soaking wet, and my kids are like, "Daddy's mad!" It's very tense, and Liz says to me, to try to defuse the tension, "Well, look at it this way, it'll be a good story." And I snarled at her, "No! Ray dropped his wedding ring down an air conditioning vent in the second episode of this season. So this isn't a story, this is just something *shitty* that happened."

When she says, "This could be a good story," it's like you saying to her, "Are you PMSing or something?"
Tucker: It's funny, when you and your wife watch any episode about a fight between Ray and Debra, a lot of times it's the first time your wife's seeing it or even hearing about it. And then you sense her eyes on you, and you don't even want to look away, and you go, "I didn't write this episode, okay? I checked out that week. I didn't write any of these jokes. You're wonderful and fantastic!"

Mike Scully: My wife had a funny idea. She said that one day they should bring all the writers' wives in to meet with Phil and tell their sides of the stories. He'd probably get another season's worth of stories. My own temptation is that if I'm going to tell a story from my real life, I'm going to try to tell it in a way that makes me look great and not accept any fault for

any stupid thing I do. In the end, you'll wind up getting a better show if there's more of a balanced conflict. There's a lot more for you to play with. If it's very one-sided—where it's very obvious to everyone that one person is right and the other is wrong—it just won't be as rich.

Aaron: I wrote a script about when Ray learns that he's not good in bed, and it was completely made up, 100 percent fabricated. My name is Aaron Shure, my very happy wife's name is Ruth.

Steve: Your very happy and satisfied wife.

Aaron: No, actually, that did come from my life. God bless Ray, there are a lot of actors who wouldn't want to be portrayed as being anything less than stellar in the sack. You know, they're happy with the *Men Are from Mars, Women Are from Venus,* I-don't-understand-romance thing, but to get it to the point where they're failing in the sex department, most actors don't usually go for that. Ray is very generous, in terms of what he's willing to play and do.

What other real-life events have wound up on the show?
Aaron: The episode where Ray tapes over the wedding video, I did that. I actually taped over ours with an episode of *Raymond,* because at the time I was trying to research the show to get hired. Ruth and I discovered it on our first anniversary. It was . . . it was . . . well, it was a lot funnier the way Ray and Patty did the scene. I think Phil hired me out of a sense of extreme pity. I can't explain why my wife is still with me.

Steve: We've established it's not the sex.

Aaron: Another example is a show I cowrote with Tom, about an answering machine tape that Ray kept of a woman breaking up with him. And I have a tape of a woman breaking up with me. It opens a lot of questions. My wife did ask, "Why do you still have that tape?"

Steve: The real tape was like twenty minutes or something.

Aaron: Yeah, it was long. Turns out she had some compelling arguments.

Leslie: The episode I wrote, "The Shower," was based on a thing that happened years ago. I was driving home from a baby shower where they served wine—I wasn't much of a drinker—and when I felt it hit me, I thought, "Do the responsible thing, pull over and park." So I park, I go to sleep, and about an hour later, two cops wake me up and take me to jail. I'm like, "But I did the right thing!" I ended up spending the night in a cell with a drunk one-armed woman who's swinging her empty sleeve around and saying, "I said to them, just try to cuff me! Just try to cuff me!" I'm thinking, "Oh, this is like a bad sitcom. And I can't even use it." So years later, when I had an opportunity to come here and pitch, I thought this was a show that could do that story without it being bad, because they would keep it about relationships. So I walked into this very room, met these guys for the first time, and thought, "I'm finally in this room, and I'm gonna tell them all that I'm a drunk."

Jeremy: It all springs out of life, out of our lives. Carl Reiner, the big daddy of the modern sitcom, *The Dick Van Dyke Show,* used to ask his writers, "What's going on in your lives? What happened this week? What happened yesterday?" We had a bird fly into our window, and it was hurt, and it took us four or five hours to track down the right place to take it. So I thought it would be nice to find out how Amy's family would react to that situation. I brought it to the room, and it was Phil who said, "Well, what if this gentle person kills the bird?" As opposed to what we had done, actually taking care of it. Very interesting! There was a truth to be found about how these people are different from the Barones. And of course, it isn't about the bird at all. The bird is simply a catalyst for people's deep anguishes and emotions and frustrations and accusations. Everything's a crucible for our torrent of rage and issues and stuff that's all flowing in the subterranean part of ourselves. It's all gotta come up.

EPISODE 95
BAD MOON RISING

PHIL: WHY IS THIS SHOW ABOUT PMS THE FAVORITE OF SO MANY PEOPLE, ESPECIALLY MARRIED PEOPLE? I'D LIKE TO GO ON RECORD SAYING THAT ALMOST EVERY STORY YOU SEE ON OUR SHOW COMES FROM SOMETHING IN OUR LIVES. EXCEPT THIS SHOW. THIS STORY WAS COMPLETELY MADE UP, AND IS A PERFECT EXAMPLE OF THE CREATIVE MIND INVENTING NOTHING BUT PURE, FANCIFUL FICTION. PUT THE LAMP DOWN, DEAR.

Ray: Although its name is "Bad Moon Rising," people always refer to this show as "The PMS Episode." Phil and I cowrote it. We've cowritten a couple. He usually writes one half, I write the other, then we fine tune 'em into one cohesive story. This was a perfect episode for two married men to write. They say comedy comes from pain and suffering — which explains why this episode turned out so funny.

Max Rosenthal and Al Romano

Having a comedian for a son isn't easy—unless you're a comedian yourself. While you might imagine that the lives of Max Rosenthal (*left*) and Al Romano (*right*) were plagued by their smart-ass sons, apparently the opposite is true. Like their mutual on-screen doppelganger, Frank, these two are full of wisecracks and practical jokes. Whether they're doing it to get laughs or "just to be mean," Max and Al aren't afraid to stir up trouble—especially when they're paid SAG wages to do so.

Max Rosenthal

What did you think when Phil told you that he wanted to write comedy?
We always told him that he had a talent for writing. But he wanted to be an actor. He wasn't interested in writing. Once we had an anniversary party for one of our friends, and we asked Phil to write something, and it was hysterical. He made fun of all the other friends there.

Did Phil misbehave growing up?
Well, he never wanted to study or anything. He wasn't a good student. We were celebrating his fortieth birthday at the Friar's Club in California, and I told everyone that we were in school as much as he was, speaking to his teachers. I said, "Although he did graduate with honors—that was Sam Honors, our neighbor's son."

Did he listen when you told him to straighten up and fly right?

No, he always had his own mind. If he didn't want to do something, you could beat him over the head ten times, but he would never do it. When my wife was yelling at him, he used to go to bed and go to sleep. He was very passive.

Do you watch the show?
I don't watch anything else. I think it's the best thing on television.

What do you think makes it work?
They have perfect timing. Sometimes the actors just stand there looking, and people laugh. As long as people laugh, they keep the camera on that person. Like Brad Garrett when he has that look, or Doris Roberts.

Do you see yourself in Frank?
When he's kiddingly insulting the wife—I do, then.

You've been on the show?
Deep down, I was always a ham actor. I wanted to be a stand-up comic when I was a kid. I did it a few times, socially, for little organizations that I belonged to, but never professionally. The great thing about being on the show is, I don't have to audition. I'm in.

Al Romano

What was Ray like growing up?
He was sort of a cutup, you know? He got into little scrapes here and there. Nothing that he would be arrested for.

I heard that you once changed Ray and Anna's outgoing answering machine message.
I'll never live that one down! I found a way that I could cancel Anna's outgoing message, so I put my own little message in there.

Were they mad?
Anna was mad. When we lived close by, I used to come and knock on the door, unannounced. She couldn't take that. She'd say, "You let me know when you're coming over." One day I pulled up in front of their house, and I had the cell phone and I said, "Anna, can I come over?" and she said, "Well, do you have to?" And I said, "Yeah, I wanna come over and see the kids." She said, "Okay." So I was parked out in front, and I just jumped out of the car and knocked on the door. She couldn't believe that I got there so quickly!

Are you a big shot among your friends, thanks to Ray?
I must've gotten well over a hundred autographed pictures for people. This one friend of mine, he sends me maybe ten or fifteen names. "Can you send an autographed picture?" So I send him twelve, fifteen pictures, and then about a month later he gives me another ten, fifteen names. He's in a retirement home, so he goes around and asks all the people in the home, "Hey, I know Ray Romano's father, you want a picture?" He asks the doctors there, too, because some of them say, "Make it out to Doctor So-and-So!" I was thinking of charging everybody two dollars for an autographed picture.

You have two other sons. Are they single, like Ray's brother used to be on the show?
No, they're both on their second marriages. I'm the only dummy! We just had our fiftieth anniversary. The secret? Be a little stupid, I guess. My wife says the secret is patience.

Do you communicate well?
Oh no, we don't communicate too well. [Mrs. Romano's voice in background] She says we're a little bit like Frank and Marie.

PHIL: A DREAM. TO COMBINE THE WORK, PEOPLE, PLACE, AND FOOD THAT YOU LOVE MOST IN THE WORLD, AND HAVE A TELEVISION NETWORK PAY FOR IT, IS A PRETTY GOOD SCAM.

Ray: I had never been to Italy, and I'll be honest, I wasn't as excited as Phil. I'm not crazy about travel and all that, and I could have done without it. So we filmed this episode about visiting our relatives and living in their charming little world for a few days and coming away with a new perspective on life and family. When we wrapped, the cast and crew went home, but my wife and I didn't. She took me to Sicily for three days to visit her hometown. It was a small village on the side of a mountain. It was absolutely life imitating art, or vice versa. It was like visiting the true-life version of what we had just fictionalized. The people, the food, the small cars, the warmth, the values, the charm. I don't like getting all sappy and emotional, so I'll stop now, but that was quite an (big word time) epiphany for this New Yorker who, to quote a line from that episode, "really wasn't interested in other cultures." Those two weeks changed my outlook on a lot of things. Okay, now beat it.

EPISODE 100
WALLPAPER

PHIL: WE DO MOST SCENES TWO, SOMETIMES THREE TIMES WHEN FILMING IN FRONT OF THE AUDIENCE. THE CAR COMING THROUGH THE HOUSE WE DID ONCE. WE'RE DOING WELL, BUT NOT WELL ENOUGH TO RIG THIS THING UP AGAIN.

AN INTERVIEW WITH DORIS ROBERTS

A mother's love for her son is a lot like a dog's loud, piercing bark: protective, loyal, and impossible to ignore. No one can blame Marie Barone for loving her son Ray so much, but one *can* blame her for some of the other crap she pulls on a regular basis. While it's true that Marie might be manipulative and nosy and meddlesome and needy, it's only because she cares so very much—so much that her family wishes she would care a whole lot less. But that's not a mother's way—particularly when that mother is Marie. Whether she's urging Amy to send a thank you note for a gift Marie herself picked out or sharing

with Debra the horrible parable of "The Big Fork and the Big Spoon," Marie moves in mysterious ways indeed.

Doris Roberts, with her low voice and self-possessed tone, has little in common with Marie. But Doris says that she has compassion for her character's predicament. With years on Broadway under her belt, she talks about comic timing, those looks that can make paint peel, and the fun of performing for a live audience.

How was your audition for Marie?
They had auditioned more than a hundred women prior to me. It took them a long

time to get to me, but okay. I was directing a play at the time. It had twenty-three people in it. I was in way over my head. Usually I spend an enormous amount of time preparing for an audition. I didn't have much time, though, so I went with my instincts, my gut reactions. It worked!

What were your first experiences with Marie?
I thought the pilot was so brilliant, and the writing was so exceptional. I had a great scene in which Ray sent his mother, as a birthday present, a Fruit-of-the-Month thing, and she had all these pears. I was hysterical over it. I mean the character was just hysterical. "What am I going to do with all these pears?" "Well, give them to Robbie." And I said, "Robbie can't eat all those pears." "Or Lee and Stan." I said, "Lee and Stan buy their own fruit." Then I find out that it's coming every month, and I get hysterical, thinking it's some kind of a club or cult. I get hysterical and start screaming, "There's too much fruit in the house!" That was an incredibly wonderful script. They all are, but I thought that one was really exceptional. I remember Les Moonves after that scene was done, saying, "That's a classic."

What do you think your contribution to the show has been?
As irritating as Marie may be, as much of a control freak and pain in the neck as she may be, and as meddlesome as she may be—it all stems from loving her children. She wants the house to be cleaner, she

wants Debra to be a better cook, she wants the children to have better food—all those things. That is not a monster kind of lady.

So you soften up the monster.
I bring in a much different lady. A different level of intelligence, a different personality, by going up to that other level of my voice. I also walk a thin line, because you never get mad at Marie. You are annoyed by her. You are exasperated by her. You are ready to kill her sometimes, but you laugh at her.

How do people react to your character?
When I walk down the street, certainly when I go back to New York, I can't go anywhere without people screaming, "Marie!" Bus drivers and cops and taxi drivers—regular people. They come at me with a smile. They are so happy to see me, because I make them laugh. If I can make them laugh, then they can laugh at their own mother or their own mother-in-law. And you don't do that in real life. Because these women, as I see them, were never taught to do anything except to get married very young, to have babies, to take care of their husbands and their children and their household. And that's great! Then the kids grow up, and when they leave, these women feel obsolete. They feel like they have no purpose any longer. Who's there to do for? Yes, you cook for your husband, but you've been doing that for forty-five years. So they get you back with food. And then they get you in front of or around that dining table and they get right in your face and tell you what to

do with your life. They really mean well. They shouldn't be doing that, but they really mean well.

That definitely comes across in your character. Marie has a lot of love to give, for all her flaws.
That's why you can laugh and go along with her, find her impossible and all those things, but funny. There's a combination of two mothers—Phil's mother is a German Jew and Ray's mother is, of course, Italian-American. So there's a difference. One mother is cerebral and one is visceral.

What is it like to play the same character for so long?
It's always different, because it's in front of a live audience. I come from theater. I did twenty-one years on Broadway before I came out here. Lily Tomlin saw me in a play called *Bad Habits* and brought me out to do her comedy special. We won Emmys for it. They picked up Howard Cosell's variety show instead of giving us a series.

How do you get along with Ray?
We have a great relationship. I think he tends to be somewhat guarded in that I represent his mother. So I don't think he would tell off-color jokes to me, whereas Brad would, and vice versa. I'll tell you, though, in these past seven years, I've watched Ray grow as an actor, and it is extraordinary. He's willing to take chances and to be courageous! I'm very proud of him, and he should be very proud of himself. But I do think he's slightly guarded,

because I have been his mother for almost eight years now.

And do you have a good rapport with Brad and the rest of the cast?
I love Brad. He's mad as can be. I play cards with him. And Patty is terrific. Peter, of course, I adore. It's like we've been married for forty-five years. It's wild. And I had never worked with him before. I knew his work certainly, and loved it. He talks about seeing me onstage in New York.

Are there any deep, dark secrets around here?
No, it's wonderful. They're all fabulous and they're all bright. We like each other, we respect each other, we laugh at each other, we find each other amusing and interesting and intelligent and all those good things. But what is most important, we really trust each other. There's no one, not one person on that set who does a star turn. Or tries to. That is so unusual and it's so gratifying. We give each other the chance to live out the character, and in so doing, it becomes hysterical.

You do seem to be having a good time on the set.
It keeps you alive. You never know what's going to happen. I know that I can give Peter a look that will really stop him in his tracks. That's great fun. And we do it in front of a live audience. That keeps me on my toes. You have to listen, you have to hear them, because they will give you the timing of the comedy.

EPISODE 107
THE SNEEZE

Ray: Here's Patty watching me show off my athletic ability. Look at how turned on she is.

CHRISTMAS PRESENT

HELEN ROSENTHAL AND LUCIE ROMANO

Good mothers give their sons unconditional love—unless they're screwing up. They support their sons' decisions—unless they disagree with them. They make their sons warm, nourishing, delicious meals—unless they don't like to cook very much.

And good mothers are humble. They don't take credit for their kids' successes. At least not publicly. Helen Rosenthal and Lucie Romano may have had their family lives paraded before millions, but these two have nothing but kind words to say about their talented, loving, considerate sons.

Of course, if mothers made good character witnesses, the streets would be teeming with criminals.

HELEN ROSENTHAL

What was Phil like growing up?
He was one of these people who marched to his own tune, and there was nothing to deter him. This was the way he wanted to do things and you could stand on your

head. This is probably a trait that serves him well now—it didn't serve me very well at the time. Because, as a mother, you expect certain things, but when he decided to do something, he did it, and when he didn't, he didn't. That is what you call passive resistance.

Did you have a clue as to what Phil was going to become?
I remember my pediatrician asking him when he was three or four, "What do you want to do?" He told her he wanted to be an actor. And the bane of my existence was that he watched television from morning to night. Now, of course, he can say that this was his homework. We tried to curtail it, but it was very difficult. That was his interest. He loved television.

Was he a show-off as a kid?
That was not his style. He liked to entertain, and he liked to be onstage, but he was never a show-off. He's more reserved than that. If you sit down with him at

dinner and he starts talking, he doesn't demand the attention, but somehow because of the way he presents the story or tells it, the attention is centered on him. He has that presence, but he does not demand it. He's very happy to have other people in the spotlight.

Do you recognize yourself in Marie?
Not in her personality, but in the situations. Philip has developed and, of course, exaggerated situations from home. The pilot, where Ray signs Marie up for a Fruit-of-the-Month Club and she hates having all that fruit in the house, is taken directly from our lives. Another episode that came from me was "The Toaster." We got a package from Philip, and we saw that it was a toaster. I said to my husband, "Why don't you exchange it and get a coffeemaker?" I really did not need the toaster. So my husband went to a department store and exchanged it for a different appliance. I hadn't had an opportunity to call Philip to tell him what I did, or even to thank him for the gift, but he called us, and I wasn't home, and he said, "Dad, did you get the toaster?" Max said, "Yes, thank you very much." So Phil said, "Wait, did you open it?" Max said, "Well, to tell you the truth, Mom didn't want the toaster, so I returned it." As he's saying that, Phil put him on speaker phone so all the writers could hear. And he said, "You mean you never took it out? Do you realize that it said 'Everybody Loves Raymond' on it?" Max almost died. He said, "I'm going back!" And he went and bought the toaster back. He knew exactly where the toaster was, and he said, "I changed my mind." Phil said, "Dad, I can just picture someone picking that toaster up, bringing it home, then bringing it back to the store and saying, 'I'd rather have a *Frasier*

toaster.'" That has taught us to open the packages. Now we have a whole museum of *Everybody Loves Raymond* appliances.

Do you give Phil feedback on the show?
We usually talk the day after a show runs. He calls to see what we thought of it or what our friends are saying. We talk about a particular thing we liked, expressions that we picked up, whatever. I work at Meals on Wheels, but as it happens, the particular program that I'm attached to is in the Dominican convent, so I work with the nuns. And the whole convent there loves the show. Every Tuesday morning when I come in, I get a report from everyone.

Where does Phil's sense of humor come from?
My husband has a good sense of humor, and *his* father had a good sense of humor. We're all used to teasing each other. Our way of communicating is always a little caustic. Our compliments come out in funny ways. In our family, there was a great deal of back and forth. Nobody ever held back in this family. We always said what we meant. Sometimes it's good and sometimes it doesn't work, but that's the way we are. We are what we are.

LUCIE ROMANO

What was Ray like growing up?
He was a good guy. Never got in trouble.

He didn't?
Starting from elementary school, he was always a cutup, and he made his teachers crazy. They always said that he was brilliant, but he just always liked to fool around, clown around. He got in trouble because he threw his hat up on the chandelier. All the teachers kept telling me, "He would do so much better if he would only knuckle down."

Were you a strict parent?
We had a lot of rules and regulations. At

the same time, I realized that, being a boy, he needed to run around and have fun, so the house was always full of kids coming in and out.

Did you think he would do something with comedy?
He was always very, very witty, but we never considered it as a career. During college, he started doing stand-up at the comedy clubs, and the comedy clubs won out over school. So he went for three years and he was on the Dean's List, but the fourth year, he didn't finish because he really made a choice. From the beginning, people liked him. When he bombed once, it discouraged him, so he dropped it for a while.

He's very hard on himself, isn't he?
He's a perfectionist! I'm a musician. I studied to be a concert pianist, so I can understand that. When you're creative and you train to perform, you have to be hard on yourself. I didn't teach that to him, but that's the way he is.

When he told you he was going to be a stand-up comic, what did you think?
Well, we were a little upset that he was quitting college, because he was in his last year. But we didn't give him a hard time. That was what he wanted to do

and needed to do, and he was already doing well.

Do you ever see yourself in any of the stories on the show?
This is going to sound funny, and I don't even know if I've voiced it in front of Raymond, but they must know it—my husband and I have that bickering back-and-forth that Frank and Marie have. And that instant forgetting. I call it a love-hate relationship. Al's not as bad as Frank is on the show. He doesn't unbuckle his pants . . . but he can be very annoying. I mentioned it once to a friend of mine. "Do you notice that Doris and I are alike in that way, that we'll get very angry with our husband and then it's over, it's finished?" When Phil started to write this, he told me that he was basing the mother more on his mother than on me.

Do you watch the show every Monday?
Oh, absolutely. That is a must. And I watch the 11:30 p.m. rerun almost every night, just before I go to sleep. We go to bed late. I like to read, and then at 11:30 I turn on the rerun, and I really get hysterical, no matter how many times I've seen it. And it makes me miss Raymond so much more!

WHAT GOOD ARE YOU?

Ray: This scene takes place in Nemo's Pizzeria and Restaurant. We named it Nemo's after the dog I had when I was sixteen — a little fun fact. Here's another: I'm allergic to pears.

PHIL: I THINK FACIAL EXPRESSION IS EVERY BIT AS
IMPORTANT TO COMEDY AS A GOOD LINE OF DIALOGUE.
BUT FEW THINGS ARE AS IMPORTANT AS BRAD GARRETT.

STEFANIA ARRIVES

PHIL: ALEX MENESES PLAYS STEFANIA. LIKE A YOUNG SOPHIA LOREN, NO? NOT EVEN ITALIAN. MEXICAN–ROMANIAN. STILL GOOD.

Ray: I can't comment on Stefania, because I'm assuming that at some point my wife will read this book. I'll just second what Phil said: Still good.

EPISODE 115
HUMM VAC

PHIL: A BIG DAY IN THE BARONE HOUSEHOLD: MARIE TAKES THE PLASTIC SLIPCOVER OFF THE SOFA. APPARENTLY, MANY OF YOU OUT THERE HAVE SOFAS THAT HAVE NEVER BREATHED FREELY. LIVE YOUR LIFE!

Ray: Plastic covers are a common thing in Italian households. Plastic-covered furniture, towels you can't touch, china no one is ever going to use. Everything in my mother's house is for a special occasion that hasn't happened yet.

EPISODE 116
THE CANISTER

PHIL: WE DON'T DO THIS STYLE OF SHOW VERY OFTEN. IT'S A "CAPER" — AN INTRICATE, FARCICAL STORY THAT BEGINS SIMPLY AND BECOMES MORE AND MORE COMPLICATED AS IT GOES. WE DON'T DO THEM OFTEN, BECAUSE THEY'RE HARD AS HELL TO WRITE. THE TRICK IS TO HAVE AS MUCH FUN AS POSSIBLE AND YET STILL HAVE SOME KIND OF EMOTIONAL RESONANCE, SOME POINT TO THE SHOW. WE'VE TRIED TO DO THAT IN EVERY EPISODE, NO MATTER HOW SEEMINGLY SILLY.

AT THE END OF THIS ONE, FRANK TAKES THE RAP FOR DEBRA. SHOCKED, DEBRA ASKS WHY HE DID THAT. HE SAYS, "BECAUSE . . . YOU'RE LIKE MY DAUGHTER."

Ray: Again, this is my favorite type of episode: small story becomes big story, I make a funny face, we go to commercial.

EPISODE 121
FRANK PAINTS THE HOUSE

Ray: This show is an example of how great our crew is. They make anything we need look real and believable. I wish they could do the same for my acting.

EPISODE 123
THE ANGRY FAMILY

PHIL: MY SON, BEN, WHO WAS SIX AT THE TIME, GETS A "SPECIAL THANKS" CREDIT AT THE END OF THIS EPISODE. HE TOLD THE STORY OF "THE ANGRY FAMILY," WHICH WAS PRESENTED HERE EXACTLY AS IT HAPPENED IN HIS FIRST-GRADE CLASSROOM. AT FIRST I WAS MORTIFIED. AND IN THE NEXT SECOND, I THOUGHT, "HOW LUCKY AM I TO HAVE A CHILD WHO WRITES FOR MY TELEVISION SHOW?"

Ray: That's my real-life wife on my right, making her silent cameo. Let's see, TV wife on one side, real wife on the other. Who should I kiss? I'm not that stupid.

EPISODE 125
ODD MAN OUT

Ray: Joking around at the end of this scene, I picked up Stefania and carried her into the house. Everyone thought it was funny, except my wife. Then I hurt my back, and my wife said, "Now it's funny."

EPISODE 127
MARIE'S
SCULPTURE

PHIL: A SCULPTURE THAT LOOKS SOMETHING LIKE THIS ONE ACTUALLY RESIDES OUTSIDE THE COURTHOUSE IN ROCKLAND COUNTY, NEW YORK, WHERE I GREW UP. I CALLED MY PARENTS TO HAVE THEM GO TAKE A PHOTO OF IT FOR ME. MOM: "PHILIP NEEDS A PICTURE OF THE VAGINA SCULPTURE." DAD: "THE WHAT?" MOM: "THE VAGINA SCULPTURE OUTSIDE THE COURTHOUSE." DAD: "THERE'S A VAGINA SCULPTURE OUTSIDE THE COURTHOUSE?" MOM: "YES! IT'S THE SCULPTURE THAT LOOKS LIKE A VAGINA! EVERYONE KNOWS IT LOOKS LIKE A VAGINA — CAN'T YOU SEE THAT?" A MOMENT, THEN . . . DAD: "WHAT DO I KNOW FROM VAGINAS?"

Ray: It's too easy to make a joke with this picture, so I'm not gonna touch it with a ten-foot . . . never mind.

AN INTERVIEW WITH MONICA HORAN

The trouble with an on-again, off-again relationship is that, by the time your flinchy loser of a boyfriend is finally ready to commit, you may be too sick of him to take him up on it. Not so with Amy. Somehow, she's so in love with Robert that she doesn't even begrudge him all of those torturous, indecisive years. In fact, she doesn't seem to begrudge him anything. We'll give it six months and then: Let the begrudging begin!

But Monica Horan appears to be just as smitten with her real-life husband, creator, show-runner, and executive producer Phil Rosenthal. In fact, she went so far as to call him a *genius.* Even after thirteen years of marriage. Even though they're raising two young kids together. Even though they *work* together *almost every day.* Sounds a little suspicious, doesn't it? We're guessing Phil hired a look-alike actress to sing his praises for this interview, while his real wife was sitting by a pool somewhere, tossing back gin-and-tonics to dull the pain.

Since you're married to Phil, I'm guessing that you've been closely involved with the show since the very beginning.
It's funny, because it's so vivid—I remember sitting up and watching *Letterman.* I always used to get a stomachache with the comedians, because I hate seeing a comedian bomb, and there had been a few in a row who weren't that great. I always get anxious for them, so it's not a really enjoyable viewing experience. I remember Ray coming on, and I was going, "Oh no! I'm nervous!" And he was really good, and I thought, "Oh, he's funny! What a relief!" We thought, "This guy's hilarious!" And then Phil told me a few months later that he'd been asked to meet him. He said, "Remember that guy we saw on *Letterman?*" That was the beginning.

How did you and Phil meet?
We met in 1986, in New York. We had gone to the same college, Hofstra University, but we didn't actually meet there. He had seen me in a play that I put together with a bunch of friends

from college. Phil knew these people, so he came to see the play, and he sent a message backstage saying, "Tell that girl she's really funny!" And I was like, "Oh my gosh, that's Phil Rosenthal!" I had heard his name, but I had never met him before. We met at the Ninth Avenue Food Festival a couple of weeks later, and the first thing he said to me was, "I'm a really big fan of yours." He was really cute! I immediately had a big crush on him. He recommended me for a little play he was doing, and I got cast in it, and that's really when we started seeing each other. He was an actor at the time.

Well, thank God that changed!
Yes, it's much more secure for all involved. I get to be an actress, and it doesn't matter if I make a dime! He came out here as an actor, and six months later, he had a job writing on a sitcom.

What's it like working with your husband so closely?
The reason that the show has the depth that it does is because of Phil. One of the best parts of being involved with this show is being able to work with him and to see him work. When he gives his notes sessions, it's such a study. I feel like I'm at the Actor's Studio or something, because he is so clear and so psychologically sound, and it's so based in the truth. Today, for instance, Ray is jumping around with a Chinese dragon on his head. But even so, nothing is frivolous. People don't say lines just for a laugh. The psychology is all revealed in the stuff that they're saying and doing. By the time we get the scripts, that has all been sorted and thought out. That level of depth comes from Phil.

Well, I would think you were blinded by love, except that the rest of the cast and writers keep repeating the same thing.

It's rare that the star of a show and the show-runner are so in sync and work so well together. It's a unique thing. That's another reason why the quality of the show is so good. Ray and Phil work together so well, and their focus is really on the scenes and on the quality of the writing and what they're communicating. They're both very focused that way.

What was your first episode?
It was called "Who's Handsome?" Robert had been single and he finally had a date and the family was all excited. My character was friends with Debra. It was just a one-episode thing in the first season, but it went really well, and Brad and I had good chemistry, so they said that they were going to bring the character back. I had fired my agent a week before. I had my son, Ben, and I wanted to have another child, and I was not liking the stuff that I was auditioning for. I had done some of my own writing, and I was doing a sketch comedy show with my friend Judy Toll, and I decided, "I don't want to audition for this crap anymore!" It was kind of a low period. And then, that week, Phil said, "I'm gonna bring you in for this part." I stopped auditioning for other things, and these episodes would come up, and they were really fun.

Your role was pretty sporadic until recently.
I never knew that it would continue, and I never asked. When Robert and Amy got engaged, everybody said, "You know what's coming!" and I never wanted to hear about it, and we didn't really talk about it at home, either. It worked very well, because I never had any drive, which I always thought was bad about me and made me a bad actress—that I wasn't driven and I didn't work hard enough. It saved me in the end, because I think our marriage would've gone down the tubes if I was this driven actress. Because if the story works, it works, and if it doesn't, Phil doesn't do it. He didn't know if I was ever coming back. Every episode could've been my last one, and that was okay with me. I was happy with what I got. And I'm grateful for that, because ten years earlier, I could've been like, "My agent is on your ass!"

So were you surprised when your role became so central?
We had just shot an episode when Phil said, "Read this." It was the script for the next week, and Robert and Amy get engaged. I felt like I was in *Stage Door* or something. I was sitting outside the studio, reading the script and crying! Part of it was that I loved the show so much and loved the characters. I felt like, "Oh my god! Amy's getting engaged!"

But it was never really a scheme of either of yours.
The network liked it. That was another thing—at the beginning, they said, "Let's bring this relationship back." Phil always tells me that Les Moonves didn't know I was his wife until a year later. He was surprised. That was my biggest compliment.

What do you think you've brought to Amy?
Phil has totally written it to me. He really uses what he sees in each person. There's such a huge element of Patty in Debra, elements of Doris in Marie, in all of us—whether people know it or not. With my character, it's a combination of my mother and me—we're very cheery people. As Amy said in a recent episode, "I come from a family that wouldn't yell if they were on fire!" When you have that characteristic next to Robert, it's just hilarious.

Those faces that you do are really funny!

Well, that's another thing—he knows that I can do that. He'll sometimes say to me, "Just do that!" Like at Robert and Amy's wedding, he said, "Don't move! Don't move. Just hold that. Don't move the whole time." Which is great, because I don't see what my face is doing. But I have a huge face—I mean, it's unbelievable. When I first started auditioning, they would say, "Well, how do you see yourself? Who are you?" and I would say, "I don't know, I feel like I change all the time." That's just what my face does. I have a rubbery face.

You have to check in the mirror just to see what your face is doing.
That's right! You don't even know what you're communicating. I had this one line, and obviously my face wasn't working, and Phil said, "What are you doing? What are you saying?" I said, "I don't know!" I'll feel like I'm giving a blank face, and then I'll see it, and it's this huge expression. And he said, *"Ya hafta know what your face is doing."*

It's fun to see how Amy's going to react to these new family situations, because she's so honest about how she feels.
Well, that's the thing. When there's no guile, and you're confronted with all that . . . it's great, because then I do get to get upset and hysterical, or get angry and all these other things. It's still the same person, but it's that person caged or backed into a corner. She's not from a background where people yell, but now she's yelling. We change because of the people we're around. But what's great about doing TV is that you get to see your character grow the way a person would.

FRANK GOES DOWNSTAIRS

PHIL: PETER BOYLE, GOD BLESS HIM, DID HIS OWN STUNT HERE. ABOUT SIX TIMES.

EPISODE 133
THE KICKER

Ray: We had to do this scene six times. I didn't mind, because between takes, like my contract says, I get to lick the icing off any appliance.

LUCKY SUIT

PHIL: WRITER TUCKER CAWLEY'S
FATHER IS AN ATTORNEY. BEFORE
AN INTERVIEW, HIS FIRM RECEIVED
AN E-MAIL ABOUT HOW THE FELLOW
THEY WERE INTERVIEWING DIDN'T
HAVE HIS "LUCKY SUIT." HIS WIFE
FORGOT TO PICK IT UP FROM THE
CLEANERS AND SENT THE NOTE TO
"HELP" HIM. IT DIDN'T TAKE LONG
TO COME UP WITH HOW THIS COULD
FIT INTO OUR LITTLE WORLD. BRAD
AND DORIS BOTH WON EMMYS FOR
THIS EPISODE.

EPISODE 140
THE BREAKUP TAPE

Ray: If you're like me, you've probably wondered, "How the hell did Ray Romano win an Emmy?" I still can't figure it out. This episode, I guess, is the answer. It had just enough humor, plus a little emotion. This is a picture of me reading a poem to Debra, because I'm jealous over a poem that her old boyfriend wrote to her years ago.

"Debra's Ears"
One on each side like a dainty cup.
So gently they hold thine sunglasses up.
So round and nice with a subtle ridge.
There's no bone in there, it's cartilage.

EPISODE 135
TISSUES

PHIL: WE DON'T DO HUGE PHYSICAL THINGS IN THE SHOW VERY OFTEN — IT'S NOT THAT KIND OF SHOW. BUT WHEN WE DO, WE LIKE TO GO ALL THE WAY. "WELL, WHAT WOULD HAPPEN IF RAY WERE ALLOWED TO START MAKING DECISIONS AROUND THE HOUSE, LIKE DECIDING WHAT BRAND OF TISSUE TO BUY?" "WELL," CONCLUDE THE WRITERS, "WE THINK HE HAS TO BURN DOWN THE KITCHEN."

LOOK AT RAY'S INADEQUATE HOSE.

Ray: A lot of episodes come from real life. I will confess that I've never actually hosed down my living room, but you see that stupid look on my face? That's real.

THE FIRST TIME

Ray: This was one of our annual year-ending flashback episodes. Thank God Andy Garcia lent me his hair for the day.

EPISODE 145
MOTHER'S DAY

PHIL: THIS STARTED AN ARC OF STORIES WHERE MARIE AND DEBRA DON'T SPEAK TO EACH OTHER. WE WANTED IT TO LAST A WHOLE SEASON, BUT REVISED THAT TO THREE EPISODES SINCE IT WOULDN'T BE MUCH OF A SHOW IF WE LEFT IT FOR THE MEN TO TALK TO EACH OTHER.

EPISODE 148
THE CULT

PHIL: *ABOUT AS OUT THERE AS WE'VE EVER GONE, BUT STILL STAYED ON EARTH. WE THOUGHT ROBERT, WITH HIS LOWER THAN AVERAGE SELF-ESTEEM, WOULD BE THE PERFECT CANDIDATE FOR A FEW MEETINGS WHERE PEOPLE BUCK HIM UP. OF COURSE, THEY'RE MORE IMPRESSED WITH HIS FAMOUS BROTHER, SO EVEN IN ROBERT'S CULT, EVERYBODY LOVES RAYMOND.*

Ray: Sherri Shepherd, who plays Robert's police partner, is always funny and makes a great addition to any episode. Here she is watching me manhandle 6'8" Brad Garrett.

EPISODE 150
HOMEWORK

PHIL: MANY TIMES, WRITERS COME INTO WORK COMPLAINING ABOUT HOW LATE THEY'D HAD TO STAY UP WITH THEIR KIDS DOING HOMEWORK. JEREMY STEVENS PROBABLY SUFFERED THE MOST, BECAUSE HE LIVED THROUGH THREE TEENAGERS. IT'S FUNNY HOW OUR PARENTS NEVER THOUGHT WE HAD TOO MUCH HOMEWORK, AND YET ALL THE PARENTS OUR AGE THINK THAT OUR KIDS DO.

Ray: In this scene on the left, I'm reacting after Peter Boyle stabs me in the hand with his fork. I hate it when he improvises.

EPISODE 154
THE SIGH

Ray: I feel bad saying this, but I'm gonna tell you the truth about the origin of this episode. Patty Heaton is the smelliest actress on television, and for years I begged the writers, "Could we please write an episode where I hose her down?" For the love of God, something had to be done...

PHIL: STEVE SKROVAN'S WIFE SIGHED ONE NIGHT WHEN THEY WERE SHARING THE BATHROOM SINK, AND STEVE GAVE HER THE BATHROOM. JUST GAVE IT TO HER. HE WENT DOWN THE HALL AND STARTED SHARING THE KIDS' BATHROOM. HE TOLD US THIS IN THE WRITERS' ROOM. WE TOLD HIM THAT, NOT ONLY WAS HE AN IDIOT, BUT THAT HE HAD TO WRITE THIS STORY. THAT'S HOW WE DO IT.

So we made up some phony story about a bathroom fight. I don't even remember what the show was about, all I remember is that for one week I could actually breathe through my nose.
(I'm kidding. Patty smells fine. She may not like what I wrote, but that's the sad truth about comedy. Somebody's gotta get hurt.)

EPISODE 156
She's The One

Ray: If you watch this episode again, try to watch this moment right here, where I yell, "She ate it!" to Brad Garrett. I had been staring so intently at his girlfriend, who I had just witnessed eating a dead fly, that when I finally screamed it to him, I actually almost fainted. If you watch closely, the moment after I scream it, while the audience is laughing, you can see me trying to remain standing. I actually dip down a little. Thankfully, the blood came back to my head and I continued the scene.

PHIL: EVEN THIS EPISODE IS BASED ON REAL LIFE. IT HAPPENED TO RAY'S BROTHER, AND IT WAS WORSE THAN WHAT WE DID. ALL I'LL SAY IS THAT, IN REAL LIFE, THEY WEREN'T FROGS, THEY WERE SNAKES.

MARIE'S VISION

PHIL: WHAT HAPPENS WHEN A PARTICULAR, FAULT-FINDING
NOSY-BODY GETS NEW GLASSES AND CAN SUDDENLY FIND
A WHOLE NEW WORLD TO CRITICIZE? RAY BLACKENS HIS
SIDEBURNS, DEBRA CRANKS THE MASCARA UP TO "RACCOON,"
ROBERT GETS A FEW BOTOX INJECTIONS — MS. ROBERTS
GETS ANOTHER EMMY.

Ray: My five-year-old likes this show because I told him
Marie was Harry Potter.

EPISODE 158
THE THOUGHT THAT COUNTS

PHIL: STARTING WITH THE "FRUIT-OF-THE-MONTH CLUB" IN THE PILOT, THE BARONE FAMILY HAS ALWAYS BEEN LOUSY AT BUYING AND RECEIVING GIFTS. HERE, FOR DEBRA'S CHRISTMAS PRESENT, RAYMOND HAS TO TOP WHAT HE GOT FOR HIS MOTHER. CLUELESS, HE ASKS ROBERT FOR ADVICE, AND FOR SOME REASON (WE WON'T SAY "OBSESSED"), ROBERT KNOWS EXACTLY WHAT DEBRA WILL LOVE. RAY BUYS IT, SHE DOES LOVE IT, AND THEN ROBERT CAN'T LIVE UNTIL SHE KNOWS IT WAS HIS IDEA. THIS IS AN EXAMPLE OF THE STORY COMING FROM CHARACTER. THE TRAITS AND BEHAVIORS OF THE CHARACTERS DICTATE THE ACTION OF THE STORY—THE STORY IS NOT SUPERFICIALLY OR GENERICALLY IMPOSED ON THEM. AND THANK YOU FOR JOINING ME FOR ANOTHER EDITION OF "TRUE BUT DULL."

Ray: We had to nail two Christmas trees together because we couldn't find one taller than Brad.

JUST A FORMALITY

PHIL: HERE'S SOME GREAT CASTING: THE INTRODUCTION OF GEORGIA ENGEL, FRED WILLARD, AND CHRIS ELLIOTT AS AMY'S FAMILY. IT'S A PRETTY BIG RISK TO MARRY OFF A REGULAR CHARACTER, A POTENTIAL "JUMP THE SHARK" MOMENT. BUT WITH THESE ACTORS, AND MY LOVELY WIFE, COMBINED WITH OUR BRILLIANT ORIGINAL CAST, WE WERE ABLE TO SEE THE POTENTIAL FOR ANOTHER SEASON OF STORIES.

EPISODE 166
SLEEPOVER AT PEGGY'S

PHIL: PEGGY "HITLER," THE COOKIE LADY, PATS RAYMOND'S
NEARLY NON-EXISTENT BOTTOM IN THIS EPISODE. ONE OF THE
REQUIREMENTS FOR SUCCESS IN HOLLYWOOD IS THAT ONE MUST
BE BOOTYLICIOUS. AND YET, EVEN THOUGH RAY WAS SADLY BORN
WITHOUT THE REQUISITE BOOTY, HE HAS SOMEHOW TRIUMPHED.

Ray: My real-life daughter, Alexandra, plays Peggy's daughter, Molly, in this episode. I think this show answers the question, "Could I possibly get any uglier?" Yes, just add water.

BAGGAGE

PHIL: *If you take anything from this book: Don't let a suitcase full of cheese be your big fork and spoon.*

Ray: Tucker Cawley won our first writing Emmy for this great episode. Like most of our stories, it was inspired by a real incident. Thank you, Tucker, and all of the writers, for taking your private and personal struggles with your loved ones and exploiting them for laughs. Your loyalty and dedication is a little sad, but greatly appreciated.

ROBERT'S WEDDING

PHIL: MOST PEOPLE HAVE TOLD US THAT THEY LIKED ROBERT AND AMY'S DANCE. MONICA AND I DID A VERY SIMILAR DANCE AT OUR WEDDING IN 1990. THE DANCE REPRESENTS JOY, LOVE, AND LAUGHTER — AND MASKS THE INABILITY TO SERIOUSLY DANCE.

Ray: These dance scenes are very difficult for an insecure person like me. The dancing's not hard — it's all the eye contact.

MADYLIN, SULLIVAN, AND SAWYER SWEETEN

Ray: When we started the show, the twins weren't actors. They were just two cute one-year-old babies. Now all you have to do is watch an episode we did this year, "Home From School," and you'll see that the boys are still cute. They're still kids. But they have become great little actors.

It's really been fun watching Madylin Sweeten grow into a fine actress. She's the same age as my daughter, and they've become close friends. I think it's because Madylin is just as sweet in real life as she is on the show.

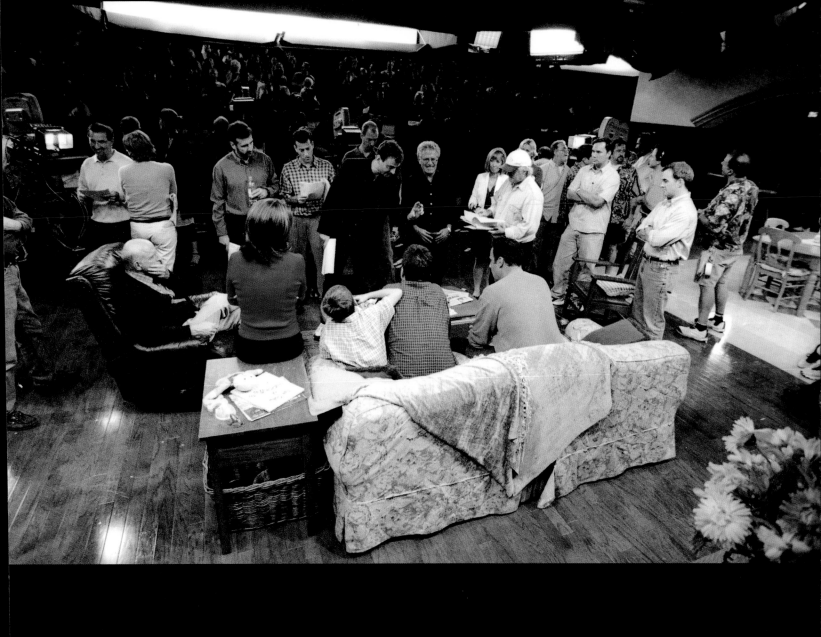

FUN WITH DEBRA

PHIL: WE HAVE A TREMENDOUS SET DESIGN AND CONSTRUCTION DEPARTMENT, BUT THEY DON'T USUALLY GET TO SHOW THEIR STUFF, BECAUSE MOST OF OUR EPISODES ARE IN THE KITCHEN. BUT IN THESE SHOTS, YOU SEE HOW IMPRESSIVE THE FAKE OUTDOORS CAN BE.

Ray: I'm a sixteen handicap in real life, but whenever Ray Barone golfs, he's a seven. That's acting.

123

EPISODE 173
THANK YOU NOTES

PHIL: AMY AND ROBERT RETURN FROM THEIR HONEYMOON AND WALK INTO A LANDMINE NAMED MARIE, WHO WANTS TO KNOW WHY THEY HAVEN'T WRITTEN THEIR THANK YOU NOTES YET. A NICE WELCOME TO THE FAMILY FOR AMY, AND ONE BASED ON A TRUE ARGUMENT THAT HAPPENED TO THE ACTRESS WHO PLAYS AMY, WHEN SHE MARRIED INTO A GANG OF MANIACS.

Ray: Phil gets very expressive and passionate when he talks to us between takes. Here he is telling us about his lunch.

HOME FROM SCHOOL

Ray: The writers are enjoying the fact that they made Ray-the-monkey dance.

EPISODE 176
THE CONTRACTOR

PHIL: THE "TABLE READ" IS THE FIRST TIME THE SCRIPT IS READ OUT LOUD BY THE ACTORS, AND IT'S THE LAST TIME IT WILL BE PERFORMED STRAIGHT THROUGH. THIS IS THE SHOW IN ITS PUREST FORM, AND USUALLY WE WON'T GET CLOSE TO THIS FEELING OF PURE THEATER AND STORYTELLING UNTIL THE EPISODE IS FINISHED AND ON TELEVISION. MAYBE WE COULD SAVE A LOT OF TIME AND MONEY AND JUST BROADCAST THE TABLE READINGS.

Ray: At table reads, Brad will try to make me laugh by looking at me with a funny face — which I find redundant.

EPISODE 175
MISERY LOVES COMPANY

PHIL: AT THE END OF THIS SHOW, MARIE GIVES THE YOUNGER BARONES
HER OWN MARRIAGE ADVICE: "WE'VE BEEN THROUGH IT ALL. AND NOW . . ."
FRANK: "WE'RE WAITING FOR DEATH." THE END. WE'VE ALWAYS FELT IT
WAS ONE OF OUR RESPONSIBILITIES TO BE UPLIFTING.

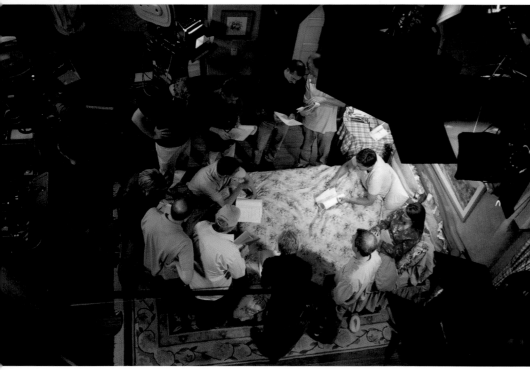

Ray: Those intimate scenes with me and Patty in the bedroom, as you can see in the between-takes shot on the left, are not so intimate. But they are still my favorite kind of scene. The comic chemistry we have (and trust me, it's 90 percent her and 10 percent me) is usually never more clear than in the bedroom scenes. I like it that there's no blocking, no business, no props — just me and her talking.

PETER ON THE COUCH

PHIL: ALL OF US HAVE BEEN BIG CHRIS ELLIOTT FANS, BACK TO WHEN HE WAS "THE GUY UNDER THE STAIRS" ON DAVID LETTERMAN.

THIS EPISODE WAS A DELIBERATE ATTEMPT TO FLESH OUT AND HUMANIZE HIS CHARACTER, AND CHRIS WAS TERRIFIC. MY PARENTS USED TO FEEL ABOUT CHRIS'S CHARACTER THE WAY FRANK AND MARIE FEEL ABOUT HIM IN THE SERIES (THIS HAPPENS A LOT). UNTIL THIS EPISODE. NOW THEY THINK HE'S CUTE.

ONE WEEK, ONE EPISODE
THE BIRD, DAY 1

9:15 A.M., PRODUCTION MEETING

It takes four days to make an episode of *Raymond*. In the weeks prior, the writers turned their fights with family and friends into a script, and in these four days, the production team will make that script a reality. At the production meeting on Stage 5 on the Warner Bros. lot in Burbank, any questions about wardrobe, props, and set design are answered.

10:00 A.M., TABLE READ

About thirty people—writers, crew, network executives—gather in the living room set to watch the cast read the script out loud for the first time. The writers listen and make check-marks next to the lines that get laughs, and make note of scenes that need more attention.

10:30 A.M., NETWORK NOTES

Immediately after the table read, executives from HBO, CBS, and Worldwide Pants gather around the table to give Phil their notes about what they think needs work. Phil then tells the director what to focus on for the day's rehearsal. Here, Georgia Engel is asking Phil a question about her role: She wants to know how to break a bird's neck.

11:45 A.M., REHEARSAL

The cast rehearses throughout the day. Meanwhile, the writers head back to the production office, on the other side of the lot, to make any changes the script might need. As the pages are finished, they are rushed down to the stage. Scripts are color-coded for each day of the production week: Monday, blue; Tuesday, pink; Wednesday and Thursday, yellow.

2:30 P.M., RUN-THROUGH FOR WRITERS

The writers head down to the stage to watch a run-through of the show. This is the first time they'll see the script on its feet. After each scene, Phil goes over the blocking and acting with the director and the actors. This is usually the toughest run-through of the week—there are so many new elements coming together, from learning lines and blocking the actors to establishing the scenes' rhythms.

4:15 P.M., WRITERS' ROOM REWRITE

After they're done onstage, the writers head back to the writers' room to rewrite any parts of the script that need it. After that work is finished, the new scripts, now pink, are messengered to the actors' and director's homes by the show's production assistants. In this picture, Ray has just been told that he has to do a whole scene with his shirt off. He thought the writers were kidding.

ONE WEEK, ONE EPISODE
THE BIRD, DAYS 2 & 3

10:00 A.M., REHEARSAL

Tuesday morning, the cast rehearses onstage. As the actors get more familiar with the material, the scenes start to take shape. But like Ray's droopy feather, certain kinks still need to be worked out.

3:00 P.M., NETWORK RUN-THROUGH

At three in the afternoon, there is a run-through for the same people who watched the table read. The actors perform the show straight through, and afterwards, there is a kind of huddle where the network execs give their notes to Phil. After that, Phil sits with all the actors to go over the scenes.

5:00 P.M., REWRITE

At the end of the day, Phil and the writers are back in the writers' room, making minor adjustments. Ray always joins these sessions when he doesn't have to be onstage. By early evening, the now-yellow scripts are messengered to the people who need them.

10:00 A.M., CAMERA BLOCKING

Wednesday is camera-blocking day, when the director and crew figure out where to position the four cameras for the best coverage. This requires the actors to stand for long periods of time—the people you see here are their stand-ins. They don't have to look like the cast, they just need to be similar in size. You can probably tell who stands in for Brad Garrett.

2:00 P.M., GREEN ROOM REHEARSAL

This is the green room, where the cast sometimes hangs out to run lines while the stand-ins are onstage. When the writers aren't on the set, they are at the production office working on future episodes.

4:30 P.M., BACK TO THE PRODUCTION OFFICE

Ray is heading to the production office after rehearsal. The camera-blocking rehearsals are taped, and at the end of the day, the tape is delivered to Phil's office. He reviews the tape with the writer of the episode and Lisa Helfrich-Jackson, who is responsible for all technical aspects of the show. The notes from this viewing are then relayed to the director and camera coordinator for the next afternoon's run-through.

ONE WEEK, ONE EPISODE
THE BIRD, DAY 4

1:00 P.M., PRE-SHOW RUN-THROUGH

Thursday is show day. The actors start rehearsing in the morning and continue until the afternoon run-through. The writers and producers watch the camera feed of the run-through on monitors just a few feet from the set. Phil and the writers then go over their notes again with the actors and director after each scene.

5:00 P.M., INTRODUCING THE CAST

During the crew's meal break, the audience is seated and entertained by comedian Mark Sweet. Around 4:00 p.m., the actors go into makeup, and at 4:30 the audience watches the episode filmed the previous week. At 5:00 p.m., Ray welcomes the audience and introduces the cast.

5:30 P.M., FILMING THE FIRST SCENE

Filming begins around 5:15. Each scene is shot twice. Last-minute adjustments are made between takes. In this picture, a professional animal handler passes a live bird to Ray. This set was built just for this episode, and will be disassembled by the end of the night.

7:00 P.M., MAKEUP ROOM REHEARSAL

There's a big scene coming up, so all the actors sit in the makeup room running lines. At the same time, Ray and Chris Elliott are getting body makeup. When they're ready, the actors take their places onstage and wait for the director to yell "Action!"

7:30 P.M., FILMING THE FINAL SCENE

The audience always laughs hardest on the first take, and their laughter is very important since the show does not use a laugh track. Also, the actors get their timing from the audience's reaction. With that in mind, the goal is to get through the first take without stopping. If anything is missed by the cameras or the actors, it's always picked up in additional takes.

8:30 P.M., CURTAIN CALL

A few minutes after the last scene is done, the actors come out for curtain call. After the show, the cast gets the script for the following week's episode. That night, the film is developed and post-production begins. It takes two more weeks of editing, color correction, and sound mixing to complete the twenty-two minutes and twenty-eight seconds of prime-time *Raymond*.

EPISODE 178
LIARS

Ray: I'll be honest, it surprised me that after one hundred seventy-seven shows, one could come along that would be one of my favorites. But this one is. The plot structure was, once again, small becomes big.

PHIL: IT'S A PRETTY FAMILY-FRIENDLY SET, AND WE'VE ALL HAD PLENTY OF KIDS SINCE THE SHOW STARTED. THAT LITTLE GIRL ON MY LAP, MY DAUGHTER, LILY, WASN'T EVEN BORN WHEN WE BEGAN THE SERIES. WE ALL BRING OUR KIDS AROUND A LOT. IT'S WONDERFUL TO SHARE THE "WORK" WITH THEM, AND HOPEFULLY THEY'LL HAVE HAPPY MEMORIES OF SEEING THEIR MOMS AND DADS DOING WHAT THEY LOVED. MY SON, BEN, JUST SAW ME WRITING THIS CAPTION AND SAID, "YOU'VE GOT IT ALL WRONG, DAD. THAT WORD, 'LITTLE,' SHOULD BE 'HORRIBLE.'"

THE SURPRISE PARTY

PHIL: I LOVED RAY'S PERFORMANCE IN THIS TEA ROOM SCENE WITH KATHERINE HELMOND. IN THE LAST SCENE, WHEN IT'S REVEALED THAT RAY DID NOTHING IN PLANNING DEBRA'S SURPRISE PARTY, IT WAS WRITTEN THAT RAY WAS SUPPOSED TO CHANGE THE SUBJECT BY PUTTING ON THE CHINESE DRAGON HEAD AND DANCING AROUND. BUT COOLER HEADS PREVAILED, AND BETWEEN TAKES ON SHOOT NIGHT, A FINAL LINE OF DIALOGUE WAS SUBSTITUTED. AMERICA WAS SPARED THE EGG ON THE DRAGON'S FACE. MAYBE YOU'LL SEE IT ON THE DVD.

Ray: The fact that Patty will do kissing scenes with me is a big ego boost. Of course, the fact that we have to put peanut butter on my lips to get her to do it is a little discouraging.

PHIL: HERE'S RAY CRACKING UP DURING A TAKE. YOU CAN'T SEE BRAD'S FACE, BUT HOW IT USUALLY HAPPENS IS: RAY MAKES WITH THE FUNNY, BRAD TRIES TO HOLD ON, LOSES, RAY LAUGHS AT BRAD. RINSE. REPEAT. WE HAVE A GAG REEL THAT WE RUN AT THE WRAP PARTY EVERY YEAR, AND IT'S FILLED WITH ALL OUR BLOOPERS LIKE THIS — WE'LL EVEN DO TAKES JUST FOR THE GAG REEL. ANYONE FROM THE OUTSIDE WHO COMES TO OUR WRAP PARTY USUALLY THINKS THAT WE THINK WE'RE HILARIOUS.

SEASON 1

#1 PILOT

Debra asks Ray to keep his parents away from her birthday party for a change. Ray agrees, but lies to his family, saying there'll be no party for Debra.

Memorable Moment: Ray has to defend his "Fruit-of-the-Month Club" gift to Marie and Frank.

Marie: "I can't talk now, there's too much fruit in the house!"

Air Date: September 13, 1996
Writer: Phil Rosenthal
Director: Michael Lembeck
Guest Cast: Stephen Lee (Leo)

#2 I LOVE YOU

Debra asks Ray why he can't say "I love you." Ray talks to his parents, trying to get to the root of his problem.

Memorable Moment: Ray asks Frank why he and Marie don't say "I love you" more.

Frank: "What, do you live in a freakin' fairyland or something?"

Air Date: September 20, 1996
Writer: Phil Rosenthal
Director: Paul Lazarus
Guest Cast: Tom McGowan (Bernie), Maggie Wheeler (Linda), Susan Varon (Suzy)

#3 I WISH I WERE GUS

Ray's Uncle Gus dies, and his will states that Ray, who fears speaking in public, is to read a eulogy. Meanwhile, Marie is upset because her estranged sister, Alda,

is coming to the funeral.

Memorable Moment: Ally draws a small, square moustache on her brother Geoffrey with a laundry marker.

Frank: "Can Hitler have a juice box?"

Air Date: September 27, 1996
Writer: Kathy Ann Stumpe
Director: Paul Lazarus
Guest Cast: Jean Stapleton (Aunt Alda), Hugh Holub (Funeral Director), Carmen Filpi (Ancient Guy), Joey Dente (Audience Member), Marlena (Member of Family)

#4 STANDARD DEVIATION

Robert gets Ray and Debra to take an IQ test. Debra scores fifteen points higher than Ray: She is in a whole other world of smarts. The next day, Robert says he made a mistake. It was actually Ray who scored higher.

Memorable Moment: Angry at the IQ revelation, Debra dumps a bowl of ice cream on Ray's lap.

Air Date: October 4, 1996
Writer: Steve Skrovan
Director: Jeff Meyer
Guest Cast: Tom McGowan (Bernie), Maggie Wheeler (Linda), Susan Varon (Suzy)

#5 LOOK, DON'T TOUCH

Ray feels guilty for being attracted to a gorgeous new waitress at Nemo's. Debra makes Ray take her there, where Ray tries too hard to appear normal.

Memorable Moment: Flustered by being so close to the cute waitress, Ray dumps an entire tray of food on Debra.

Air Date: October 11, 1996
Writer: Lew Schneider
Director: Jeff Meyer
Guest Cast: Tom McGowan (Bernie), Tina Arning (Angelina), Joseph V. Perry (Nemo), Susan Varon (Suzy)

#6 FRANK THE WRITER

After *Reader's Digest* publishes one of Frank's funny stories, he starts to consider himself a writer. To Ray's horror, Frank asks him to pass a sample column on to his editor.

Memorable Moment: An elderly Japanese couple in a Tokyo dentist's office laugh at Frank's *Reader's Digest* story.

Air Date: October 18, 1996
Writer: Tucker Cawley
Director: Paul Lazarus
Guest Cast: Yunoka Doyle (Babysitter), Kotoko Kawamura (Japanese Woman)

#7 YOUR PLACE OR MINE

After a fight with Frank, Marie moves in with Ray and Debra. Soon, Marie takes over as "Mommy," and Ray realizes that her mothering has turned him back into a child.

Memorable Moment: Ray and Robert fight over who gets the prize in a box of cereal, and Robert ends up spinning around with Ray clinging to his back.

Air Date: October 28, 1996
Writer: Jeremy Stevens
Director: Howard Storm

#8 IN-LAWS

Debra's pretentious parents meet the Barones for dinner at a fancy restaurant. Tensions rise, and Ray finally explodes, saying that the two families shouldn't be allowed to be in the same state.

Memorable Moment: Ray yells at his in-laws: "You like to make jokes about 'herbs' that nobody gets and you go to 'France' and you go to [banging silverware] 'Stomp' and you go to some basement in the Village to watch some transvestite carve a yam into a monkey!"

Air Date: November 1, 1996
Writer: Phil Rosenthal
Director: Alan Kirschenbaum
Guest Cast: Robert Culp (Warren), Katherine Helmond (Lois), Wayne C. Dvorak (Maître d'), Richard Stegman (Gerard)

#9 WIN, LOSE OR DRAW

Ray loses $2,300 to Frank playing poker. Debra tells him to ask for the money back, but Ray is too proud to do it.

Memorable Moment: Debra tries to convince Ray to get the money back.

Debra: "Ray, you know, in case you haven't noticed, we have three kids to put through college."

Ray: "Well, maybe we'll get lucky and they won't be college material."

Air Date: November 8, 1996
Writer: Kathy Ann Stumpe
Director: Alan Kirschenbaum
Guest Cast: Joseph V. Perry (Nemo), Len Lesser (Garvin), Victor Raider-Wexler (Stan), Murray Rubin (Eddie)

#IO TURKEY OR FISH

Debra wants to cook fish for Thanksgiving instead of turkey and, thinking Marie is hoping she'll fail, goes into high gear to prepare dinner.

Memorable Moment: Ray puts Debra's fish in the dishwasher.

Air Date: November 22, 1996

Writer: Tucker Cawley
Director: Michael Lembeck
Guest Cast: Robert Culp (Warren), Katherine Helmond (Lois), Phil Leeds (Mel), Pearl Shear (Emma)

#II CAPTAIN NEMO

The Nemo's basketball team elects Robert over Ray to be captain. Ray is upset, and Debra wonders why he needs to spend so much time away from his family.

Memorable Moment: Ray's teammates burst in on him while he's in the shower, and Kevin James does a dead-on impersonation of Ray: "Hey, nice nipples."

Air Date: December 13, 1996
Writers: Lew Schneider, Steve Skrovan
Director: Michael Lembeck
Guest Cast: Andy Kindler (Andy), Kevin James (Kevin), Dave Attell (Dave), Tom Paris (Tom)

#I2 THE BALL

Ray is hurt when Frank admits that the signed Mickey Mantle baseball he gave Ray as a child is a fake. Ray swears he'll never lie to his kids. Later, Ally asks if there is a Santa Claus, and Ray struggles for the right answer.

Memorable Moment: After finding out Frank signed the baseball himself so Ray wouldn't be disappointed, Ray gives his dad a kiss on the head.

Air Date: December 20, 1996
Writer: Bruce Kirschbaum
Director: Jeff Meyer
Guest Cast: Andy Kindler (Andy)

#I3 DEBRA'S SICK

Debra is sick and asks Ray to help with the kids, but he's supposed to have a meeting with Terry Bradshaw. Later, Ally and Michael get sick, too, and Ray has to take them to the doctor's office, where he has asked Bradshaw to meet him.

Memorable Moment: At the doctor's office, Ray realizes that he has brought the wrong twin. Robert then enters and, without a word, exchanges twins.

Air Date: January 3, 1997
Writer: Stephen Nathan
Director: Michael Lembeck
Guest Cast: Terry Bradshaw (Himself), Jack Blessing (Dr. Hammond), Cynthena Sanders (Parent #1), Jonathan Chapin (Parent #2), Hannah Swanson (Little Kid), Curtis Blanck (Staring Kid)

#I4 WHO'S HANDSOME?

Debra introduces Robert to her friend Amy. He makes a date with her, but later becomes self-conscious over his appearance. Ray is shocked when Debra stops just short of saying that Robert is the most handsome of the Barones.

Memorable Moment: Ray tries to fix himself up with new clothes, hair gel, and a tan.

Debra: "Ray, you're completely out of your mind. I say one thing about your brother and you turn into George Hamilton."

Air Date: January 17, 1997
Writer: Carol Gary
Director: Howard Storm
Guest Cast: Monica Horan (Amy)

#15 THE CAR

Ray buys his dad's old Plymouth Valiant. The car quickly breaks down, and Debra wants to get rid of it, but Ray insists he can fix it. Later, Robert mentions that the Valiant is the car Ray first got lucky in.

Memorable Moment: In a flashback, as Ray tries to make out with his high school crush, Robert stops by the car and ends up getting his Afro caught in the window.

Air Date: January 31, 1997
Writer: Lew Schneider
Director: Howard Storm
Guest Cast: Kristin Bauer (Lisa Constanine)

#16 DIAMONDS

Ray is shocked to learn that the engagement ring he bought for Debra with Frank's help is a fake. He has to snatch her fake diamond, hoping to replace it.

Memorable Moment: Debra wakes up as Ray tries to slide the ring off her finger using butter and a flashlight.

Ray [caught]: "Hi. [meekly] Wanna play baker in the mineshaft?"

Air Date: February 7, 1997
Writer: Kathy Ann Stumpe
Director: Michael Lembeck
Guest Cast: Monica Horan (Amy), Barry Bonds (himself)

#17 THE GAME

When the cable goes out, the family decides to play Scruples. The game quickly degenerates into a brawl.

Memorable Moment: Debra and Marie suggest that the couples talk to each other.

Marie [turning to Frank]: "We haven't had a conversation in thirty-five years."

Frank: "I didn't want to interrupt."

Air Date: February 21, 1997
Writer: Tucker Cawley
Director: Jeff Meyer
Guest Cast: Jon Manfrellotti (Cable Guy)

#18 THE RECOVERING PESSIMIST

Ray wins the Sports Writer of the Year Award, but thinks that all this means is that something bad now has to happen to him. When Frank and Marie are unimpressed, Ray realizes that his pessimism comes from his parents.

Memorable Moment: To show Ray he's a pessimist, Debra asks him to say the first word that comes into his head.

Debra: "Beach."
Ray: "Sunburn."
Debra: "Marriage."
Ray: "Counselor."
Debra: "Bad."
Ray: "Worse."
Debra: "Steak."
Ray: "Stroke."
Debra: "Sex."
Ray: "Twins."

Air Date: February 28, 1997
Writer: Steve Skrovan
Director: Jeff Meyer
Guest Cast: Marv Albert (Himself), Katarina Witt (Herself), Tom Paris (Announcer)

#19 THE DOG

A bulldog follows Ray home. He decides to give it to Robert because when they were kids, the family had to get rid of Robert's bulldog because of Ray's allergies. Later, the dog's owner shows up to claim him.

Memorable Moment: When Robert and the dog see each other from across the room, their eyes meet and it's love at first sight.

Air Date: March 3, 1997
Writer: Bruce Kirschbaum
Director: Rod Daniel
Guest Cast: Kristi Yamaguchi (Herself), Patience Cleveland (Phyllis)

#20 NEIGHBORS

The neighbors come to Ray and Debra's to complain about Frank and Marie's obnoxious behavior. Frank and Marie arrive during the meeting and get angry with Ray for betraying the family.

Memorable Moment: The neighbors show Ray a secret video montage of Frank coming out to get the morning paper in a towel, which falls off.

Air Date: March 10, 1997
Writer: Jeremy Stevens
Director: Jeff Meyer
Guest Cast: Lance E. Nichols (Mack), Cathy Ladman (Lilly), Steven Hack (Arthur), Patricia Belcher (Ruth), Don Perry (Priest)

#21 FASCINATIN' DEBRA

Dr. Nora, a phone shrink, comes to interview Debra for a book she's writing. However, she becomes more fascinated with the Barone family than with Debra.

Memorable Moment: Robert touches potato chips to his chin before eating them.

Dr. Nora: "Do you do that all the time?"
Robert: "Do what?"

Air Date: March 17, 1997
Story: Kathy Ann Stumpe, Lew Schneider
Writers: Jeremy Stevens, Tucker Cawley
Director: Jeff Meyer
Guest Cast: Mary Kay Adams (Dr. Nora), Desmond Howard (Himself), Lorraine Shaw (Bartender)

#22 WHY ARE WE HERE?

Debra asks Ray why they ever left their old apartment. Flashback three years earlier . . . Frank tells Ray and a pregnant Debra about the perfect house—right across the street from Frank and Marie.

Memorable Moment: While looking for a house, Ray maps out for Debra the perfect distance for them to live from his parents. Ray [pointing at the spot on the map]: "It's too close for an overnight. Too far for sauce."

Air Date: April 7, 1997
Writers: Ray Romano, Tom Caltabiano
Director: Jeff Meyer

SEASON 2

#23 RAY'S ON TV

Ray's first TV appearance, on the show *Sportscall,* is a disaster. Ray's second appearance is even worse.

Memorable Moment: Frank, after watching Ray mispronounce "cinnamon" on TV: "I could've eaten a box of Alpha-Bits and crapped a better interview."

Air Date: September 22, 1997
Writer: Tucker Cawley
Director: Michael Lessac
Guest Cast: Kevin James (Kevin), Andy Kindler (Andy), Roy Firestone (Himself), James Worthy (Himself), Ana Gabriel (Stage Manager)

#24 FATHER KNOWS LEAST

Ray and Debra take a class, "Parenting Effectiveness Training," and learn a new technique called "Active Listening."

Memorable Moment: Ray tries "Active Listening" on Debra. Debra's response: "Don't give me that Active Listening crap. Where do you get off listening to me?"

Air Date: September 29, 1997
Writer: Lew Schneider
Director: Michael Lessac
Guest Cast: Linda Kash (Celia)

#25 BROTHER

It's the two-year anniversary of Robert's divorce, and Marie and Frank convince Ray to spend the evening with his brother. But Ray fears that he'll have to spend the night listening to Robert talk about his feelings.

Memorable Moment: Robert keeps pressuring Ray to share his personal life, until Ray blurts out that the first time he slept with Debra, he cried. Robert feels that's too personal.

Air Date: October 8, 1997
Writer: Jeremy Stevens
Director: Michael Lessac

#26 MOZART

Ray wants Ally to take piano lessons with Marie, but Ally is not receptive to this idea. Ray takes a piano lesson from Marie, hoping to inspire his daughter.

Memorable Moment: Marie gives Raymond a piano lesson and is mortified when he remembers very little. Eventually, Ray relearns enough to play the theme from *Love Story.*

Air Date: October 13, 1997
Writer: Phil Rosenthal
Director: Ellen Gittelsohn

#27 GOLF

Ray tricks Debra into letting him play golf, but then has a panic attack in the locker room. Ray's doctor tells him to relieve stress by playing more golf.

Memorable Moment: Marie tells Debra that there's a very simple way she can help Ray

relax.

Marie: "Are you making yourself available to him?"
Debra: "Please, Marie!"
Marie: "You know Raymond doesn't like to ask for things."

Air Date: October 20, 1997
Writers: Ray Romano, Tom Caltabiano, Kevin James
Director: Ellen Gittelsohn
Guest Cast: Kevin James (Kevin), Iqbal Theba (Dr. Sundram)

#28 ANNIVERSARY

On Frank and Marie's fortieth anniversary, they fight, and Frank says the only good year out of forty was the year he left Marie. Flashback to 1967, where we see why Frank left . . . and why he returned.

Memorable Moment: Ray learns that he's the reason his parents got back together, and he feels guilty because if they had stayed apart, they might have met other people and had happier lives.

Debra: "Think of your parents as a terrible virus. If they had met other people, the misery would have spread."

Air Date: October 27, 1997
Writer: Kathy Ann Stumpe
Director: Ellen Gittelsohn
Guest Cast: Phil Leeds (Uncle Mel), Monica Horan (Amy), Daniel Hansen (Young Ray), Ethan Glazer (Young Robert)

#29 WORKING LATE AGAIN

Debra brings Ray dinner at the office and finds him goofing off, playing paper football. Debra gets Ray to start working from home.

Memorable Moment: Ray receives a fax of his friend Dave's buttocks. His mother doesn't like that.

Air Date: November 3, 1997
Writers: Ellen Sandler, Cindy Chupack
Director: Will Mackenzie
Guest Cast: Andy Kindler (Andy), Dave

Attell (Dave), Christopher Michael Moore (Guy), Pat O'Brien (Himself)

#30 THE CHILDREN'S BOOK

When Ray tries to help Debra write a children's book, they end up with two different versions and decide to let Ally choose which one is better.

Memorable Moment: Frank shows Ray and Robert a nude portrait he painted of Marie long ago.

Air Date: November 10, 1997
Writer: Steve Skrovan
Director: Will Mackenzie

#31 THE GIFT

Ray gets caught off-guard when Robert buys Frank an impressive TV "Remote Boat." So Ray decides to buy Frank a fancy tropical fish aquarium.

Memorable Moment: Overshadowed by Ray once again, Robert stares through the giant aquarium.

Air Date: November 17, 1997
Writers: Ellen Sandler, Cindy Chupack
Director: Will Mackenzie
Guest Cast: Andy Kindler (Andy), John Lee (Wo-Hop)

#32 HIGH SCHOOL

Ray goes to his high school reunion and ends up with the nerds, while Debra hangs with the popular crowd.

Memorable Moment: Ray, feeling sensitive about having to wear ear plugs for medical

reasons, speculates that Debra might have had cool medical problems.

Debra: "No, I never ruptured my booty. One time I did sprain my groove thing."

Air Date: November 24, 1997
Writer: Lew Schneider
Director: Gary Halvorson
Guest Cast: Bob Odenkirk (Scott Preman), Brian Posehn (Warren), Pamela Bowen (Jessica Bell), Marty Rackham (Pete Hastings), Andrew Williams (Cool Guy)

#33 THE LETTER

After Marie ruins Debra's Tupperware party, Debra sends Marie an angry letter.

Memorable Moment: In front of the shocked family, Frank reads Debra's letter out loud, then says to Debra, "You're my favorite writer."

Air Date: December 8, 1997
Writer: Kathy Ann Stumpe
Director: Gary Halvorson
Guest Cast: Monica Horan (Amy), Maggie Wheeler (Linda), Andy Kindler (Andy) Nora Dunn (Helen), Kristen Trucksess (Gayle), Jon Manfrellotti (Gianni)

#34 ALL I WANT FOR CHRISTMAS

It's Christmastime, and Ray tries repeatedly to get Debra "in the mood," but he keeps getting thwarted. Debra finally tells Ray that he's sexiest when he's just being himself.

Memorable Moment: Ray: "Now? You're in the mood now? It's Christmas, my parents are coming over . . ."

Debra: "So?"
Ray: "So, you've activated the launch sequence."

Air Date: December 15, 1997
Writer: Steve Skrovan
Director: Jeff Meyer
Guest Cast: Andy Kindler (Andy), Christine Cavanaugh (Erin)

#35 CIVIL WAR

Ray learns that Frank is taking Robert to a Civil War reenactment and manipulates Frank into asking him to go, too. Ray confesses that he just wanted to be close to his father.

Memorable Moment: During the "war," Ray gets "killed" almost immediately and has to spend the rest of the weekend as a "corpse."

Air Date: January 5, 1998
Writer: Tucker Cawley
Director: Gary Halvorson
Guest Cast: John O'Donohue (Harry)

#36 MIA FAMIGLIA

Ray and Ally track down the Barones' oldest living relative: Aunt Sarina in Italy. Three weeks later, Aunt Sarina shows up at their door and transforms the Barone family.

Memorable Moment: The Barones laugh and sing at the dining room table, before realizing that this wonderful woman is not related to them.

Air Date: January 12, 1998
Writers: Ellen Sandler, Cindy Chupack
Director: Brian K. Roberts

Guest Cast: Argentina Brunetti (Zia Sarina), Stella Farentino (Anna Barone), Phil Leeds (Uncle Mel), Mike Batay (Cab Driver), Vito D'Ambrosio (Language Teacher)

#37 MARIE'S MEATBALLS

Marie teaches Debra her recipe for meatballs, but Ray hates them. Later, Debra discovers that Marie switched spices on her.

Memorable Moment: Debra peels off the label on the bottle of sage Marie gave her and sees that it's actually tarragon.

Debra [screaming]: "Who's the nutcase now, Ray? Who's the nutcase now?!"

Air Date: January 19, 1998
Writer: Susan Van Allen
Director: Brian K. Roberts

#38 THE CHECKBOOK

Ray takes over the family finances, and within six weeks they're in financial hell.

Memorable Moment: Through the bank window, Debra sees Ray and Robert causing a scene at the ATM machine.

Air Date: February 2, 1998
Writer: Tom Caltabiano
Director: John Fortenberry
Guest Cast: Andy Kindler (Andy), Tina Arning (Angelina), Joseph V. Perry (Nemo), Martha Faulkner (Old Lady), Richard Romano (Senior Officer)

#39 THE RIDE-ALONG

Ray goes on a ride-along in Robert's squad car. That night, Ray gets to see Robert foil a holdup at Nemo's.

Memorable Moment: Confronted with the realities of Robert's job, Marie reveals her true feelings for him.

Air Date: February 23, 1998
Writer: Jeremy Stevens
Director: John Fortenberry
Guest Cast: Sherri Shepherd (Judy), Tina Arning (Angelina), Joseph V. Perry (Nemo), Susan Varon (Suzy), Stephen Bruno (Hold-up Guy), Bruce Nozick (Dispatcher)

#40 THE FAMILY BED

Ray won't let Ally sleep in their bed. Debra always has to go to be with Ally in her room, but now it's Ray's turn. Ray gets Marie to secretly do it for him.

Memorable Moment: To Debra's surprise, Marie enters Ray and Debra's bedroom with her face covered in cold cream, followed by Frank, who declares he can't sleep without his "Great Wall of Marie."

Air Date: March 2, 1998
Writer: Steve Skrovan
Director: Steven Zuckerman

#41 GOOD GIRLS

Marie admits she likes Amy more than Debra because she's a "good girl," i.e., virginal, just like Marie was before marriage. Competing with Robert, Ray lies to his mother, telling her that Debra was also a good girl.

Memorable Moment: Marie reveals she was pregnant with Robert before she and Frank got married, and that they've been lying about Robert's birthday.

Marie: "We were young and in love."
Frank: "I wanted sex."

Air Date: March 9, 1998
Writer: Tucker Cawley
Director: Joyce Gittlin
Guest Cast: Monica Horan (Amy)

#42 T-BALL

Ray and Debra fail to bring an approved snack to T-ball, and Debra refuses to knuckle under to pressure from the other parents.

Memorable Moment: Ray screams at mild-mannered T-ball coach Bryan Trenberth.

Air Date: April 6, 1998
Writer: Lew Schneider
Director: Jeff Melman
Guest Cast: Dan Castellaneta (Bryan Trenberth), Jenny Buchanan (Lisa Trenberth), Jerry Hauck (Parent), Yolanda Snowball (Teacher)

#43 TRAFFIC SCHOOL

Robert teaches traffic school with the aid of his ventriloquist dummy partner, Traffic Cop Timmy.

Memorable Moment: Robert [as Traffic Cop Timmy] to Frank: "Remind me not to drive with you, you crazy bastard."

Frank [rising to fight]: "What'd you say to me?" Ray [to Frank]: "Dad, puppet."

Air Date: April 20, 1998
Writer: Kathy Ann Stumpe
Director: John Fortenberry

#44 SIX FEET UNDER

Ray discovers that he is "five-eleven and three-quarters," though he thought he was six feet tall. This triggers a midlife crisis, and upon making a list of his goals, Ray decides there's nothing to look forward to and becomes obsessed with death.

Memorable Moment: Ray: "Write the great American novel? I don't even want to read the great American novel."

Air Date: April 27, 1998
Writers: Cindy Chupack, Steven Skrovan, Tom Caltabiano
Director: Jeff Melman
Guest Cast: Andy Kindler (Andy), Kevin James (Kevin), Jon Manfrellotti (Gianni)

#45 GARAGE SALE

At the family garage sale, faced with selling the crib and baby clothes, Ray isn't so sure that he and Debra are done having kids. By the end of the sale, Ray is convinced they're done, but Debra isn't so sure.

Memorable Moment: Marie admits that she always wanted a daughter.

Marie: "I used to put Robert in a little pink dress and dance him around the room."

Later, Robert discovers a photo and yells: "Ray? Ray? Tell me we have a sister!"

Air Date: May 4, 1998
Writers: Ellen Sandler, Jeremy Stevens, Lew Schneider, Tucker Cawley
Director: Jeff Melman
Guest Cast: Nick Degruccio (Wendell), Susan Segal (Pregnant Woman), Richard Marion (Don), Sarah Rush (Woman)

#46 THE WEDDING, PART I

In a flashback, we see Ray's marriage proposal to Debra via his newspaper column. After she accepts, Ray worries that Debra felt compelled to say yes because his family was there, or that she just wants a wedding.

Memorable Moment: Frank reads Ray's first published column, becomes angry with Ray for how it reflects on him, and remains furious all the way through Ray's heartfelt, printed proposal to Debra.

Air Date: May 11, 1998
Writers: Ray Romano, Phil Rosenthal
Director: Jeff Melman
Guest Cast: Robert Culp (Warren), Katherine Helmond (Lois), Andy Kindler (Andy), Kevin James (Kevin)

#47 THE WEDDING, PART II

After a flashback to the days leading up to their wedding, Ray fears Debra doesn't love him, but just wants a wedding, and he gets cold feet.

Memorable Moment: Robert, the best man, concludes his toast by touching his champagne glass to his chin. All the guests then do the same.

Air Date: May 18, 1998
Writers: Ray Romano, Phil Rosenthal
Director: Jeff Melman
Guest Cast: Robert Culp (Warren), Katherine Helmond (Lois), Charles Durning (Father Hubley), Fred Stoller (Gerard), Phil Leeds (Uncle Mel), Kristen Trucksess (Bridesmaid #1), Elizabeth Herring (Bridesmaid #2), Sarah J. Hale (Bridesmaid #3), Al Romano (Lewis), Michael Duddie (Duddie), Kevin James (Kevin), Andy Kindler (Andy), Tom McGowan (Bernie)

SEASON 3

#48 THE INVASION

Ray and Debra stay with Frank and Marie while their house is being fumigated.

Memorable Moment: Ray has to share a bed with Robert. Ray: "Hey, could you put a shirt on?" He slides in next to Robert. "And some underpants?" Later: "C'mon, a guy gets into bed with you, you put some pants on."

Air Date: September 21, 1998
Writer: Ellen Sandler
Director: Will Mackenzie
Guest Cast: Matthew Kimbrough (Exterminator) Philippe Benichou (TV Announcer)

#49 DRIVING FRANK

Frank hits Robert's patrol car, so Ray tells Frank he can't drive the kids until he retakes his license test.

Memorable Moment: Ray, a licensed driver, has to accompany Frank to the DMV. On a harrowing ride, Frank shows Ray his special hand signals.

Air Date: September 28, 1998
Writer: Cindy Chupack
Director: Will Mackenzie
Guest Cast: Eddie Barth (Man)

#50 THE SITTER

Ray and Debra hire the perfect babysitter, but the kids end up liking her too much.

Memorable Moment: Marie, who replaces the babysitter, gets hurt and is lying on the couch when Robert enters with food from Nemo's for her.

Marie [taking a breadstick]: "These seem old."

Frank: "You are what you eat."

Marie: "Oh? Robbie, give your father his order of miserable bastard."

Air Date: October 5, 1998
Writer: Lew Schneider
Director: Will Mackenzie
Guest Cast: Senta Moses (Lisa), David Hunt (Bill Parker), Elizabeth Herring (Carrie Parker), Tess Oakland (Sally Parker)

#51 GETTING EVEN

Ray, the auctioneer for a school's benefit, makes several jokes about the jewelry box Debra made for the event. Upset, she vows to get even.

Memorable Moment: Frank and Marie take the canoe trip Frank won at the auction. As Marie babbles away, Frank sets her adrift without a paddle.

Air Date: October 12, 1998
Writer: Steve Skrovan
Director: Steve Zuckerman

#52 THE VISIT

Debra's mother comes for a visit and, from the moment she arrives, complains and insists on spending time away from the family—even considering checking into a hotel. Debra is deeply hurt.

Memorable Moment: Ray, Robert, and Frank, hiding from Marie, devour an entire chocolate cake as her voice plays on the answering machine.

Air Date: October 19, 1998
Writer: Susan Van Allen
Director: Richard Marion
Guest Cast: Katherine Helmond (Lois)

#53 HALLOWEEN CANDY

Ray considers a vasectomy, but instead returns home with multicolored condoms, telling Debra that the "stuff" will now be his responsibility.

Memorable Moment: On Halloween night, Frank runs out of candy and ends up giving out the colorful condoms by mistake.

Air Date: October 26, 1998
Writer: Steve Skrovan
Director: Steve Zuckerman
Guest Cast: Andy Kindler (Andy), Tina Arning (Angelina), Jospeh V. Perry (Nemo), Susan Varon (Suzy), Elizabeth Herring (Carrie Parker), Tess Oakland (Sally Parker), Vinnie Buffolino (Dracula Trick-or-Treater), Ben Rosenthal (Boy)

#54 MOVING OUT

Ray and Debra tease Robert about not having his own apartment, so he moves out . . .

and moves in with an older couple who are exact replicas of Frank and Marie.

Memorable Moment: A stressed-out Ray returns home and starts getting a back rub from the woman he thinks is Debra. He gets into it—and then very quickly out of it—as he discovers the person rubbing his back is Marie.

Ray: "Oh my God, now the dreams are gonna start again."

Air Date: November 2, 1998
Writer: Tucker Cawley
Director: Will Mackenzie
Guest Cast: Monica Horan (Amy), Anna Berger (Rita Stipe), David Byrd (Harry Stipe)

#55 THE ARTICLE

Andy asks Ray to read an article he has written, and Ray gives him a lot of criticism and several suggestions. Later, Andy thanks Ray and says *Sports Illustrated* bought his article, which he submitted without including any of Ray's suggestions.

Memorable Moment: Andy's article is rewritten by the editor at *Sports Illustrated*.

Ray: "Yeah, but they bought it, right? They must've liked something."

Andy: "Apparently they liked that it was about sports. They just didn't like the words I picked or the order I put them in."

Air Date: November 9, 1998
Writer: Tom Caltabiano
Director: Will Mackenzie
Guest Cast: Andy Kindler (Andy)

#56 THE LONE BARONE

Ray vents to Robert about how miserable he is in his marriage and tells Robert that he's lucky to live alone. Later, Robert breaks up with Amy. Everyone blames Ray.

Memorable Moment: Ray: ". . . Men do that, they joke around about stuff like marriage. Right, Dad?"

Frank: "I don't know what you're talking about."

Ray [desperate]: "C'mon, like when you joke about how you wish a big tidal wave would come and sweep Ma out to sea."

Frank: "I have never been more serious about anything in my entire life."

Air Date: November 16, 1998
Writers: Tom Caltabiano, Jeremy Stevens
Director: Will Mackenzie
Guest Cast: Monica Horan (Amy), Kevin James (Doug Heffernan)

#57 NO FAT

It's Thanksgiving, and Frank and Marie have high cholesterol, so Marie makes a tofu turkey. Ray, behind Marie's back, orders a complete holiday dinner.

Memorable Moment: Marie brings out the tofu turkey.

Robert: "How 'bout that, huh? Look how it jiggles."

Ray: "That's the sign of a good bean curd bird."

Frank: "May I have my carving knife, please?"

Marie: "Thank you, Frank."

Frank: "I wanna slit my throat."

Air Date: November 23, 1998
Writers: Ellen Sandler, Susan Van Allen
Director: Steve Zuckerman
Guest Cast: Joe Durrenberger (Delivery Man)

#58 THE APARTMENT

Robert's new apartment building is full of incredibly gorgeous women, so Ray starts making lame excuses to go visit him. When Debra comes by, she discovers why Ray has been going so often.

Memorable Moment: At Robert's apartment, two sexy women mistake Debra, who is bringing over some linens, for Robert's housekeeper.

Air Date: December 7, 1998
Writer: Kathy Ann Stumpe
Director: Steve Zuckerman
Guest Cast: Janelle Paradee (Sandy), Betsy

Monroe (Michelle), Kelly Rebecca Walsh (Jessica)

#59 THE TOASTER

Ray buys the family engraved toasters for Christmas. Everybody loves them, except Frank and Marie, who return theirs for a coffeemaker.

Memorable Moment: At the department store, Frank and Marie argue as they strategize about how to get Ray's toaster back.

Frank: "Can't you just be quiet?"

Marie: "Don't you tell me to be quiet. I have a mind of my own, you know. I can contribute. I'm not just some trophy wife."

Frank: "You're a trophy wife? What contest in hell did I win?"

Air Date: December 14, 1998
Writer: Phil Rosenthal
Director: Steve Zuckerman
Guest Cast: Robert Culp (Warren), Katherine Helmond (Lois), P. B. Hutton (Exchange Lady), Peggy Doyle (Elderly Woman), Drenda Spohnholtz (Leann), Philip Abrams (Sales Clerk)

#60 PING-PONG

Ray and Robert reminisce about how Frank tortured them while playing ping-pong, until the day twelve-year-old Ray finally beat him. When Marie says that Frank let him win, Ray demands a rematch.

Memorable Moment: Frank and Ray trash-talking while playing ping-pong. Frank [getting ready to serve]: "Zero serving zero, Ray can kiss my rear-o." Then: "One serving zip, I see a quivering lower lip." Then: "Two serving nada, I'm ashamed to be his fadda."

Air Date: January 11, 1999
Writer: Aaron Shure
Director: Will Mackenzie

#61 PANTS ON FIRE

Frank and Marie find a beer bottle cap that Ray admits came from a party he threw one weekend back in high school. Marie is shocked that Ray would have lied to her and thrown a party behind her back. Upset with Ray, she starts favoring Robert.

Memorable Moment: In a flashback, we see teenage Ray's beer party.

Air Date: January 18, 1999
Writer: Tucker Cawley
Director: Will Mackenzie
Guest Cast: Bradley Warden (Drunk Kid)

#62 ROBERT'S DATE

Judy invites Robert out with all her black friends, and Robert, feeling awkward, starts acting like a black person.

Memorable Moment: Robert shows up at Ray's house wearing a yellow suit.

Frank [to Robert]: "I'm talking to you on the phone the other day? I can't even understand what the hell you're sayin' anymore. What did you call me 'dog' for?"

[Later] Ray: "Hey."

Frank: "Hey, Ugly!"

Ray: "What's that all about?"

Frank: "That's 'Robert talk.' That means you're good-lookin'." [Puts his arm around Marie] "Hey, Good-lookin'."

Air Date: February 1, 1999

Writer: Jeremy Stevens

Director: Will Mackenzie

Guest Cast: Sherri Shepherd (Judy), Shelley Robertson (Sareesa), Kivi Rogers (Man #1)

#63 FRANK'S TRIBUTE

Frank's lodge votes him "Man of the Year." Ray and Robert interview lodge members for a tribute video. But no one really likes Frank, so Ray doctors the video.

Memorable Moment: Frank, in a rare, tender moment, wipes away the tears and cold cream from Marie's cheek.

Frank: "I like you better without that crap on your face."

Air Date: February 8, 1999

Writer: Eric Cohen

Director: Will Mackenzie

Guest Cast: Len Lesser (Garvin), Victor Raider-Wexler (Stan), Charles C. Stevenson, Jr. (Milt), John David Conti (J. R. Abe), T. R. Richards (Guy), Fred Ornstein (Man #1), Greg Lewis (Man #2), Lou Charloff (Man #3), Allan Lurie (Man #4),

Jack Axelrod (Man #5), John Spaulding (Man #6), Ancel Cook (Man #7), Stuart Gold (Man #8), Al Eben (Man #9), Murray Rubin (Man #10)

#64 CRUISING WITH MARIE

Ray and Robert buy their parents a cruise for Marie's birthday, but Frank hurts his knee, so Ray is forced to go with his mom.

Memorable Moment: Injured Frank is in the hot tub, ordering Robert around.

Frank: "I am the father. You are the son. The son must serve the father."

Robert: "Oh yeah? You want to be served? [turning up the heat] Alright, I'll serve ya. But first, I'm gonna cook ya!"

Air Date: February 15, 1999

Writers: Steve Skrovan, Susan Van Allen

Director: Richard Marion

Guest Cast: Hiram Kasten (Ted), Jack Betts (Walter), Bobbie Norman (Thelma), Sharon Houston (Mary Beth Yaroush), Beecey Carlson (Merry Widow #1), Leigh Rose (Merry Widow #2), Jean Sincere (Merry Widow #3), Edrie Warner (Merry Widow #4)

#65 RAY HOME ALONE

Ray is home alone for the weekend, but he can't sleep because he's afraid. When Robert has similar troubles, he and Ray blame Frank and his scary bedtime stories. They decide to give him a good scare, hiding in his closet and waiting.

Memorable Moment: Their plan backfires when they hear Frank and Marie enter, about to have sex.

Air Date: February 22, 1999

Writers: Tom Caltabiano, Tucker Cawley, Ray Romano

Director: Steve Zuckerman

Guest Cast: Kevin James (Doug), Andy Kindler (Andy), Jon Manfrellotti (Gianni), Leslie Windram (Aileen)

#66 BIG SHOTS

Ray takes Robert to Cooperstown to meet the '69 Mets. Ray tries to cut in line using his press pass, causing a scene and getting both of them thrown out.

Memorable Moment: Robert takes off his shoes in the car.

Ray: "We must've just hit a skunk who crawled out of the ass of another skunk."

Air Date: March 1, 1999

Writers: Jason Gelles, Mike Haukom

Director: Steve Zuckerman

Guest Cast: Chip Heller (Police Officer), Gene Arrington (Security Guard), D'Wayne Gardner (Man #1), Harry Freedman (Man #2), John Fairlie (Man #3), Valerie DeKeyser (Waitress), Tommie Agee (Himself), Jerry Grote (Himself), Bud Harrelson, (Himself), Cleon Jones (Himself), Ed Kranepool (Himself), Tug McGraw (Himself), Art Shamsky (Himself), Ron Swoboda (Himself)

#67 MOVE OVER

Debra likes to cuddle with Ray in bed, but Ray can't sleep that way. Their priest advises Ray that she probably needs more affection during the day.

Memorable Moment: When Debra rolls over at night, Ray places a blow-up

clown in his place and sleeps on her side of the bed.

Air Date: March 15, 1999
Writer: Kathy Ann Stumpe
Director: Will Mackenzie
Guest Cast: Charles Durning (Father Hubley), Tess Oakland (Sally Parker)

#68 THE GETAWAY

Ray, though afraid of alone time with his wife, reluctantly agrees to go on a bed-and-breakfast weekend with her.

Memorable Moment: Ray: "You're boring? What about me? Come on, I ran out of things to say on the George Washington Bridge. Remember, I said, 'I always take the upper level, because if it collapses, you fall on the people on the lower level.'"

Air Date: April 5, 1999
Writer: Cindy Chupack
Director: Steve Zuckerman
Guest Cast: Monica Horan (Amy), Lynn Milgrim (Cecily), Rick Hall (Bill), Beth Skipp (Pam)

#69 WORKING GIRL

Debra lands a job as a copywriter, but Ray

isn't very supportive. However, when Debra gets fired, Ray goes to get her job back.

Memorable Moment: Ray [to Debra]: "You're surrounded by Barones. It's a jungle here. Survival of the fittest. If you didn't know how to hold your own, my mom would be wearing you as a coat."

Air Date: April 26, 1999
Writers: Cindy Chupack, Kathy Ann Stumpe
Director: Michael Zinburg
Guest Cast: Julie Hagerty (Charlotte Sterling)

#70 BE NICE

Ray and Debra realize that they treat everyone else better than they treat each other and vow to remedy the situation.

Memorable Moment: Marie: "My high school yearbook, Frank? I want this."

Frank: "Well I don't want it in the house. It's depressing."

Marie: "What are you talking about? I look beautiful in those pictures."

Frank: "That's what's depressing."

Air Date: May 3, 1999
Writer: Lew Schneider
Director: Steve Zuckerman
Guest Cast: Mary Jo Keenen (Lori), Stephanie Erb (Elise), Jonny Solomon (Father #1), Jerry Lambert (Father #2)

#71 DANCING WITH DEBRA

Robert needs a swing dancing partner, so Ray suggests Debra. They have a great time and make another date, but Ray, jealous, sabotages it by telling Robert that Debra didn't have fun.

Memorable Moment: Ray frantically tries to

dance away from an irate Debra and Robert, to the tune of "Sing, Sing, Sing."

Air Date: May 10, 1999
Writers: Aaron Shure, Steve Skrovan
Director: Brian Roberts
Guest Cast: Jon Manfrellotti (Gianni), Jill Zimmerman (Kristen)

#72 ROBERT MOVES BACK?

After Robert and Amy have sex at his apartment, they learn that the entire building saw them in the act. Robert, ashamed, crashes in Ray's basement.

Memorable Moment: Marie walks in on them in the basement at the wrong moment. Amy runs upstairs wearing only Robert's police pants.

Air Date: May 17, 1999
Writers: Lew Schneider, Aaron Shure

Director: Brian Roberts
Guest Cast: Monica Horan (Amy), Laurence Lejohn (Man #1), Rich Battista (Man #2), John Harnagel (Man #3), Shari Shaw (Woman #1)

#73 HOW THEY MET

A flashback to when Ray and Debra first meet. He delivers a futon to her apartment, and she invites him to dinner.

Memorable Moment: Their first kiss. When Ray inadvertently knocks Debra to the floor with the refrigerator door, he bends down to grab her—and she grabs him.

Air Date: May 24, 1999
Writers: Ray Romano, Phil Rosenthal
Director: Gary Halvorson
Guest Cast: Jon Manfrellotti (Gianni)

SEASON 4

#74 BOOB JOB

An acquaintance informs Debra that she had a boob job and shows off her new breasts. Debra asks Ray if she needs an enlargement, and when he comes home from a weeklong road trip, it seems obvious that she did it.

Memorable Moment: Debra [after taking socks out of her bra]: "I've had three children! These are not just for show! These were working breasts!"

Air Date: September 20, 1999
Writer: Lew Schneider
Director: Will Mackenzie
Guest Cast: Meeghan Holaway (Cheryl Kaler)

#75 THE CAN OPENER

Ray and Debra fight over a new can opener. Eventually, they apologize and make up, but they get mad again when Frank, Marie, and Robert get involved.

Memorable Moment: Frank and Marie fight over a can of fat.

Air Date: September 27, 1999
Writers: Aaron Shure, Susan Van Allen
Director: Will Mackenzie

#76 YOU BET

Frank starts spending more time with Ray, which Ray finds nice, but odd. Ray realizes his father's been spending time with him to get inside information for his sports bets.

Memorable Moment: Ray sets a trap for Frank with some false information.

Air Date: October 4, 1999
Writers: Ellen Sandler, Steve Skrovan
Director: Will Mackenzie
Guest Cast: Len Lesser (Garvin), Victor Raider-Wexler (Stan), John Del Regno (Sal), Monty Hoffman (Dominic), Tony Pope (Announcer)

#77 SEX TALK

When Debra reads a book on how to talk to kids about sex, it leads to unwanted revelations about Frank and Marie's sex life.

Memorable Moment: Marie: "This whole subject is improper. What we do in our bedroom is our own business, and I'd prefer not to be known as 'The Whore of Lynbrook!'"

Frank: "We can move from Lynbrook."

Air Date: October 11, 1999

Writers: Tod Himmel, Lisa K. Nelson
Director: Will Mackenzie

#78 THE WILL

Ray and Debra make out a will and must decide who will get custody of the children if they die at the same time. They agree on their friends Bernie and Linda.

Memorable Moment: The reaction of both Marie and Robert when they find out that they weren't chosen for custody of the kids.

Air Date: October 18, 1999
Story: Jennifer Crittenden, Michael Feldman
Writer: Jennifer Crittenden
Director: Will Mackenzie
Guest Cast: Tom McGowan (Bernie), Maggie Wheeler (Linda), Gary Grossman (Mr. Atkins)

#79 THE SISTER

Debra's sister, Jennifer, comes to visit. She's the black sheep of the family, and now she's becoming a nun and going on a mission to South Africa. Debra is upset and thinks it's just her sister's newest phase.

Memorable Moment: Ray gets caught by Jennifer as he is singing "Dominique," with his shirt pulled up like a nun's habit. He quickly covers his nipples with his fingers.

Air Date: October 25, 1999
Writer: Kathy Ann Stumpe
Director: Will Mackenzie
Guest Cast: Ashley Crow (Jennifer)

#80 COUSIN GERARD

Ray hires his cousin Gerard to help edit his book, but Gerard soon drives him crazy. When Ray tells Debra that his cousin is incompetent, negative, and talks in a nasal voice, she points out that Ray and Gerard are a lot alike.

Memorable Moment: Ray, face-to-face with Gerard, tries to alter Gerard's nasal voice.

Air Date: November 8, 1999

Writers: Jason Gelles, Mike Haukom
Director: Will Mackenzie
Guest Cast: Fred Stoller (Gerard)

#81 DEBRA'S WORKOUTS

Ray can't figure out why he's had sex three days in a week. He finds a brochure with a picture of Debra's hot new aerobics instructor, and thinks he's the reason Debra's been having more sex with him.

Memorable Moment: Ray [confronting Debra]: "Yeah, but that guy . . ."

Debra: "That guy just teaches class, that's all."

Ray: "That's all?"

Debra: "That's it. You know, I've . . . I've seen good-looking men before."

Ray: "Where?"

Air Date: November 15, 1999
Writers: Tom Caltabiano, Ray Romano, Mike Royce
Director: Will Mackenzie
Guest Cast: Andy Kindler (Andy), Jon Manfrellotti (Gianni), Mark Dobies (Nick), Joseph V. Perry (Nemo), Susan Varon (Suzy), Kimberly James (Monique)

#82 NO THANKS

Debra tries to change Marie's attitude toward her by responding to all of Marie's cutting remarks by being extra nice.

Memorable Moment: Ray explains to Debra how he copes with his family.

Ray: "It's like getting into a hot bath. You know, at first it's so hot that you don't think you can take it. But then . . . you know, once you get your luggage in, it's not that bad."

Air Date: November 22, 1999
Writers: Tucker Cawley, Jeremy Stevens
Director: Will Mackenzie
Guest Cast: Monica Horan (Amy)

#83 LEFT BACK

Ray has a hard time accepting that one of the twins might have to stay in pre-K an extra year.

Memorable Moment: Ray wakes up Debra in bed. Ray: "Am I stupid?"

Debra: "If this is your new way of asking for sex, then yes."

Air Date: November 29, 1999
Writer: Phil Rosenthal
Director: Will Mackenzie
Guest Cast: Diana-Maria Riva (Sarah), Monica Horan (Amy)

#84 THE CHRISTMAS PICTURE

Ray's Christmas gift to his parents is a Barone family portrait. Debra's parents unexpectedly show up at the photography studio, and Marie clearly doesn't want them there.

Memorable Moment: While she petulantly sits in a chair, an exasperated Ray slides a reluctant Marie across the floor and into the group photo.

Air Date: December 13, 1999
Writer: Lew Schneider
Director: Will Mackenzie
Guest Cast: Robert Culp (Warren), Katherine Helmond (Lois), Lew Schneider (Steven Golden)

#85 WHAT'S WITH ROBERT?

When Robert breaks up with Amy again, the family begins to wonder if he might be gay.

Memorable Moment: Frank: "Do you dust, too? With the little feather duster, Nancy?"

Ray: "You know, Dad, sometimes when you talk like that people could get offended."

Frank: "Offended by what?"

Ray: "Nothin', nothin', forget about it."

Frank: "What?"

Ray: "Nothing. It's just . . . when you say 'Nancy,' what are you implying, exactly?"

Frank: "That your name should be Nancy."

Ray: "And when you say 'Nancy,' that's your word for 'gay.'"

Frank: "Very well."

Ray: "And . . . and you mean that as an insult."

Frank: "Yes, I believe I do."

Ray: "Well, that's . . . that's not nice."

Frank: "That's why it's a good insult."

Air Date: January 10, 2000
Writer: Cindy Chupack
Director: Will Mackenzie
Guest Cast: Monica Horan (Amy), Geoff Stults (Mailman)

#86 BULLY ON THE BUS

Ray and Debra are surprised to learn that the bully on Ally's school bus is . . . Ally.

Memorable Moment: Ray, telling Debra that he wouldn't have liked her in school: "Standing in your little groups, making fun of the kid whose mom showed up with his snowpants."

Debra [laughs]: "Snowpants."

Ray: "There was a good chance of snow!"

Air Date: January 17, 2000
Writer: Tucker Cawley
Director: Will Mackenzie
Guest Cast: Ja'net Du Bois (Dottie), Cody Morgan (Todd Feeney), Andre Jamal Kinney (Kid #1), Tommy Aquino (Kid #2), Steffani Brass (Girl at Bus Stop)

#87 PRODIGAL SON

Ray gets upset when Ally draws a picture of Ray in Hell, because Frank told her that's where Ray is going if he doesn't start attending church.

Memorable Moment: Ray wants Frank to talk to Ally. Ray: "Go . . . go over there right now and tell her that I'm not going to Hell."

Frank: "You know, I would love to, but I don't make the rules."

Air Date: January 31, 2000
Writer: Steve Skrovan
Director: Will Mackenzie
Guest Cast: Charles Durning (Father Hubley), Len Lesser (Garvin), Victor Raider-Wexler (Stan)

#88 ROBERT'S RODEO

When Ray cancels plans with him, Robert picks up an extra shift and ends up getting gored by a bull.

Memorable Moment: Ray changes the bandage on Robert's "backside." Later, as Ray and Robert watch TV, CBS News broadcasts footage of Robert being chased down a street by the bull.

Air Date: February 7, 2000
Writer: Jennifer Crittenden
Director: Will Mackenzie
Guest Cast: Monica Horan (Amy), Sherri Shepherd (Judy), Christy L. Medrano (Nurse), Dana Tyler (Anchorwoman)

#89 THE TENTH ANNIVERSARY

When Ray and Debra play their wedding video on their anniversary, they discover Ray has taped a Super Bowl game over it.

Memorable Moment: Debra [hitting Ray]: "Where is my wedding, Ray?! I want my wedding!"

Air Date: February 14, 2000
Writer: Aaron Shure
Director: Will Mackenzie
Guest Cast: Robert Culp (Warren), Katherine Helmond (Lois), Andy Kindler (Andy), Jon Manfrellotti (Gianni), Charles Durning (Father Hubley), Monica Horan (Amy), Fred Stoller (Gerard), Maggie Wheeler (Linda), Sarah J. Hale (Party Guest #1), Kristen Trucksess (Party Guest #2)

#90 HACKIDU

Ray accidentally trades away Ally's valuable and rare fantasy game card, and to rectify the mistake, ends up having to contend with Amy's weird brother, who owns a comic-book store.

Memorable Moment: The Hackidu song: "High on Hackidu Mountain, where the flames shoot forth in the night / Comes the source of the Hackidu power / The power of justice and might. Buy 'em, buy 'em, Hackidu. Buy 'em, buy 'em, buy 'em, buy 'em, buy 'em, Hackidu!"

Air Date: February 21, 2000
Writers: Lew Schneider, Steve Skrovan
Director: Will Mackenzie
Guest Cast: Paul Reubens (Russell), David Hunt (Bill Parker), Scotty Leavenworth (Tyler Parker)

#91 DEBRA MAKES SOMETHING GOOD

Debra makes braciole and Ray can't get enough of it. Later, she finds out that Ray makes fun of her braciole at work.

Memorable Moment: Frank: "Anyone who can make braciole like this deserves a whole hillside full of heavenly scented marigolds and daffodils."

Air Date: February 28, 2000
Writer: Kathy Ann Stumpe
Director: Will Mackenzie
Guest Cast: Andy Kindler (Andy)

#92 MARIE AND FRANK'S NEW FRIENDS

Debra and Ray encourage his parents to make friends, but the plan backfires when Frank and Marie and their new friends, the Stipes, hang out at Ray and Debra's house.

Memorable Moment: Debra: "What do you mean, you don't have time for friends?"

Marie: "Well, after you and Raymond

moved in, I mean, I guess someone had to help you raise a family."

Air Date: March 20, 2000
Writer: Mike Royce
Director: Steve Zuckerman
Guest Cast: David Byrd (Harry Stipe), Anna Berger (Rita Stipe), Dom Irrera (Seth Stipe)

Ray: "Yeah, that's good, Ma. Now it smells like a cow died in a whorehouse."

Air Date: May 1, 2000
Writer: Tucker Cawley
Director: Steve Zuckerman

#95 BAD MOON RISING

Debra yells at Ray in front of his friends. He blames PMS, and his friends offer advice on how Ray should handle Debra's mood.

Memorable Moment: Frank: "Before you know it, what used to be a bad mood becomes her only mood. And then you become like me, where not a day goes by that I don't wish a comet was screamin' towards earth to bring me sweet relief."

Air Date: May 8, 2000
Writers: Ray Romano, Phil Rosenthal
Director: David Lee
Guest Cast: Andy Kindler (Andy), Jon Manfrellotti (Gianni)

#96 CONFRONTING THE ATTACKER

On Robert's first day back to work, he freezes up when he has to confront some teenagers. Robert decides to quit the force.

Memorable Moment: At a petting zoo, Robert confronts the bull that gored him. Robert [to bull]: "I had to move back in with my parents. That's right."

Air Date: May 15, 2000
Writers: Kathy Ann Stumpe, Lew Schneider
Director: Brian Roberts
Guest Cast: Monica Horan (Amy),

#93 ALONE TIME

Debra announces that she needs some alone time. Ray starts to wonder why, so he spies on her.

Memorable Moment: Ray, spying on Debra through their living room window, is interrupted by the mailman.

Air Date: April 17, 2000
Writer: Jennifer Crittenden
Director: Steve Zuckerman

#94 SOMEONE'S CRANKY

Robert, recovering from being gored by a bull, is staying at Frank and Marie's. They admit that Robert is driving them crazy, so Robert moves back to his apartment.

Memorable Moment: When the family goes to visit him, Robert's apartment smells of spoiled milk. Marie attempts a fix:
Marie: "I have my perfume."

Richard Assad (Candy Store Owner), Alex Solowitz (Teenager)

#97 ROBERT'S DIVORCE

While out to dinner, the Barones see Robert's ex-wife, Joanne, at another table. The scene flashes back five years earlier, and we see why she and Robert got divorced.

Memorable Moment: Debra: "Robert, I . . . I think what your father is trying to say is that sometimes Joanne is . . ."
Frank: "A nutcracker."

Air Date: May 22, 2000
Writers: Tucker Cawley, Jennifer Crittenden, Steve Skrovan
Director: Wil Shriner
Guest Cast: Monica Horan (Amy), Suzie Plakson (Joanne)

SEASON 5

#98 & 99 ITALY

Marie surprises her family with a trip to Italy. Ray spends much of the time complaining, while Robert falls in love with the beautiful Stefania.

Memorable Moment: Aunt Colleta gives Ray a bath. Later, while touring Rome, Marie interrupts an argument between Ray and Debra.
Marie: "Don't fight here, it's the Colosseum."

Air Date: October 2, 2000
Writer: Phil Rosenthal
Director: Gary Halvorson
Guest Cast: Silvana DeSantis (Aunt Col-

letta), Pierrino Mascarino (Uncle Giorgio), Alex Meneses (Stefania Fogagnolo), David Proval (Signore Fogagnolo), Sergio Sivori (Italian Man #1), Vanni Bramati (Italian Man #2), Luca Francucci (Kid #1), Alessandro Francucci (Kid #2), Rosario Coppolino (Pizza Guy), Francesca Lonardelli (Italian Woman #1), Anna Maria Senatore (Italian Woman #2), Enzo Vitagliano (Bocce Player), Carlo Piantadosi (Puppeteer)

#100 WALLPAPER

Frank and Marie's car comes crashing into Ray and Debra's living room.

Memorable Moment: After the crash, the passenger door opens, and Frank emerges. Then, the driver side opens, and Marie steps out. They look around.

Ray: "Hey."

Air Date: October 9, 2000
Writer: Lew Schneider
Director: Gary Halvorson
Guest Cast: Patricia Belcher (Ruth), Annie Abbott (Louise)

#101 MEANT TO BE

Robert's complicated love life now involves three women: his ex-wife, Joanne, the Ital-

ian beauty, Stefania, and Amy. He decides Amy is the one, but first he must tell her about the other two.

Memorable Moment: Amy climbs onto the couch to slap Robert. Then she does it again.

Air Date: October 16, 2000
Writers: Jennifer Crittenden, Kathy Ann Stumpe
Director: Michael Zinberg
Guest Cast: Monica Horan (Amy), Suzie Plakson (Joanne), Susan Varon (Suzy), David Proval (Signore Fogagnolo)

#102 PET CEMETERY

While the family is away for the weekend, Ray loses Ally's pet hamster. Robert eventually finds it in the freezer.

Memorable Moment: Ray and Robert at the freezer.

Ray: "What? All I see is fudge pops."
Robert: "Look at the hairy one on the left."

Air Date: October 23, 2000
Writer: Steve Skrovan
Director: Ken Levine

#103 THE AUTHOR

Ray's dream of publishing a book is crushed at the exact moment that Robert gets a promotion.

Memorable Moment: Ray and Robert get so mad at each other that they wrestle in the living room. Robert takes off his shoe, sticks it in Ray's face, and shouts, "Smell it!"

Air Date: October 30, 2000
Writer: Mike Royce
Director: Andy Ackerman

#104 THE WALK TO THE DOOR

Ray finds out that Elizabeth, a girl from high school, will be at an upcoming wedding. Ray explains that he didn't walk her to the door after a dance, and that this is something he has always regretted.

Memorable Moment: Ray [to Debra]: "You deserve all the love that would fit in the ocean."

Marie [to Frank]: "Why can't you say something like that?"

Frank: "Alright. I would love it if you were in the ocean."

Air Date: November 6, 2000
Writer: Tucker Cawley
Director: Asaad Kelada
Guest Cast: Vicki Juditz (Elizabeth Garini), Rudy Moreno (Nice Man), Fred Ornstein (Elderly Man), Judson Crowder (Scott)

#105 THE YOUNG GIRL

In public, Debra says it's fine that Robert is dating a very young woman. In private, she tells Ray that she is disgusted.

Memorable Moment: Debra drags a reluctant Ray out the door by his ear.

Air Date: November 13, 2000
Writers: Tom Caltabiano, Aaron Shure
Director: Michael Zinburg
Guest Cast: Tinsley Grimes (Erica)

#106 FIGHTING IN-LAWS

Debra's parents are visiting for Thanksgiving. Ray overhears Warren and Lois and discovers that they are going to marriage counseling. When Ray tells Debra, they debate whose parents are worse.

Memorable moment: Debra [to Ray]: "You listen—if my parents burned down an orphanage on Christmas Eve, they wouldn't be as bad as your parents!" She then drops the Thanksgiving turkey on to the floor, slips around, and slams it into the oven.

Air Date: November 20, 2000
Writer: Kathy Ann Stumpe
Director: Michael Zinburg
Guest Cast: Robert Culp (Warren), Katherine Helmond (Lois)

#107 THE SNEEZE

After a guy at the airport sneezes right in Ray's face, Debra must deal with his hypochondria.

Memorable Moment: The look on Ray's face when his mother, preparing to take his temperature, tells him to turn over.

Air Date: November 27, 2000
Writers: Aaron Shure, Steve Skrovan
Director: Ken Levine
Guest Cast: Andy Kindler (Andy), Jon Manfrellotti (Gianni), Bob Joles (Guy)

#108 CHRISTMAS PRESENT

Ray wants permission to golf, so he tries to bribe Debra by getting her a better Christmas present than she gets him.

Memorable Moment: Debra: "I love my pots. I'm gonna try 'em out right now."

Marie: "Well, I better go help her. They're not magic pots."

Air Date: December 11, 2000
Writer: Kathy Ann Stumpe
Director: Gary Halvorson

#109 WHAT GOOD ARE YOU?

After Debra nearly chokes on some food and Ray provides no real help, Ray wonders if anyone thinks of him as useful.

Memorable Moment: In an attempt to prove he can remove a splinter, Ray chases Debra and drags her across the living room floor.

Air Date: January 8, 2001
Writer: Jennifer Crittenden
Director: Ken Levine
Guest Cast: Andy Kindler (Andy), Jon Manfrellotti (Gianni), Robert Ruth (Nemo), Susan Varon (Suzy)

#110 SUPER BOWL

Ray takes Gianni instead of Debra on a work trip to the Super Bowl. When Ray gets there, he finds that all his coworkers have brought their wives, and it's only a matter of time until Debra finds out.

Memorable Moment: To prove his love for Debra, Ray rips up the tickets and spends Super Bowl Sunday in bed, watching the game with her . . . and Gianni.

Air Date: January 29, 2001
Story: Joe Bolster, Ray Romano, Mike Royce
Writers: Ray Romano, Mike Royce
Director: Gary Halvorson
Guest Cast: Jon Manfrellotti (Gianni), Marla Frees (Mary Jo), Timothy Durkin (Stu), Edward James Gage (Doug), J. J. Boone (Lori), Amy Janon (Hotel Clerk), Robert Romano (Rich), Melissa Beyeler (Lisa)

#111 RAY'S JOURNAL

Ray discovers that Marie read his childhood journal, and that she still bears a grudge

about some of the things he wrote.

Memorable Moment: Marie: "Fine. That's just fine, Raymond. But let me tell you something. You may have written that diary, but I had to read it!"

Air Date: February 5, 2001
Writer: Jennifer Crittenden
Director: Kenneth R. Shapiro

#112 SILENT PARTNERS

At dinner, Ray and Debra realize that they have nothing to say to each other. Worried about their marriage, Debra suggests they do more things together.

Memorable Moment: During Valentine's Day dinner at a fancy restaurant, Ray and Debra struggle to keep the conversation going by talking about bread and butter.

Air Date: February 12, 2001
Writer: Tucker Cawley
Director: Gary Halvorson
Guest Cast: Eric Ramirez (Waiter)

#113 FAIRIES

Ray finds out that Debra signed the boys up to be fairies in the school play. He's not pleased, and tries to get them better parts as

mighty boulders.

Memorable Moment: Frank catching Ray showing the boys how to fly around like pixies with wings.

Air Date: February 19, 2001
Writer: Aaron Korsh
Director: Gary Halvorson
Guest Cast: Diana-Maria Riva (Sarah), Matthew Duddie (Father), Isaiah Griffin (Josh), Matthew Romano (Lion Kid)

#114 STEFANIA ARRIVES

Marie arranges a surprise visit from Robert's Italian girlfriend, Stefania. She, in turn, surprises everyone by bringing her scary father and the news that they are moving to America. And Robert finds that, despite her womanly charms, Stefania is annoying.

Memorable Moment: When Stefania's father demands to know why Robert broke up with her, Robert explains that he is a homosexual.

Air Date: February 26, 2001

Writers: Tucker Cawley, Lew Schneider
Director: Gary Halvorson
Guest Cast: David Proval (Signore Fogagnolo), Alex Meneses (Stefania Fogagnolo), Robert Ruth (Nemo), Susan Varon (Suzy)

#115 HUMM VAC

Against Debra's wishes, Ray buys a new Humm Vac Esprit. At first, Debra is impressed with it, but she is angered when Marie explains that she sent the saleswoman over. Debra takes the vacuum to Marie's, determined to find dirt in her house.

Memorable Moment: Marie, to prove her family is more important than a clean house, agrees to let everyone sit on the couch without the plastic slipcover.

Air Date: March 19, 2001
Writer: Lew Schneider
Director: Gary Halvorson
Guest Cast: Tricia O'Kelley (Carol Marshall), David Proval (Signore Fogagnolo)

#116 THE CANISTER

Marie insists that Debra has not returned one of her kitchen canisters. Debra denies it and demands an apology. Marie gives one and leaves, but then Ally enters holding the canister. Ray and Debra try to sneak the canister back into Marie's house.

Memorable Moment: The look on Ray and Debra's faces when, after throwing the canister out, it comes bouncing back down the stairs.

Air Date: April 9, 2001
Writer: David Regal
Director: Gary Halvorson

#117 NET WORTH

Ray lends a friend money against Debra's wishes, and they argue over who should have control of the finances, and over who is "worth" more.

Memorable Moment: Debra presents Ray a bill for all the work she does.

Air Date: April 23, 2001
Writers: Jason Gelles, Mike Haukom
Director: David Lee
Guest Cast: Bob Odenkirk (Scott), Brian Posehn (Walter)

#118 LET'S FIX ROBERT

To his horror, Robert finds out that Amy and Stefania are at Marco's Restaurant trashing him. Later, he goes over to his mother's and is further horrified to learn that Marie has invited the same women over to discuss everything that's wrong with him.

Memorable Moment: Robert: "Marco's has delicious food, and now it's a gathering place for everyone who hates me."
Frank: "No wonder it got such good reviews."

Air Date: April 30, 2001
Writers: Jennifer Crittenden, Mike Royce
Director: Gary Halvorson
Guest Cast: David Proval (Marco Fogagnolo), Alex Meneses (Stefania Fogagnolo), Sherri Shepherd (Judy), Monica Horan (Amy)

#119 SAY UNCLE

Robert has plans to take the kids to the zoo. When Ray notices the kids imitating their Uncle Robert, he becomes insecure and tells Robert to get his own life.

Memorable Moment: Robert, in an attempt to get his own life, ends up in a hot tub with two women who think he's a doctor.

Air Date: May 7, 2001
Writer: Aaron Shure
Director: Kenneth R. Shapiro
Guest Cast: Michelle Beauchamp (Lisa), Renee Faia (Colleen)

#120 SEPARATION

Debra gets a surprise visit from her mother, who explains that she and Debra's father are splitting up after forty years. Debra worries that she and Ray are on the same path.

Memorable Moment: Ray, while receiving the sad news from Debra, tries desperately to restrain his impulse to laugh.

Air Date: May 14, 2001
Writer: Phil Rosenthal
Director: Asaad Kelada
Guest Cast: Robert Culp (Warren), Katherine Helmond (Lois)

#121 FRANK PAINTS THE HOUSE

Marie, desperate to get Frank out of her hair, makes him paint Ray and Debra's house. When Ray and Robert get sucked into helping their father, Frank's barking so upsets Ray that he finally fires him.

Memorable Moment: Robert accidentally power-paints Marie's face.

Frank [walking by]: "That's gonna need another coat."

Air Date: May 21, 2001
Writer: Scott Buck
Director: David Lee

#122 ALLY'S BIRTH

While accompanying Ally to a father/daughter dance, Ray reminisces about the circumstances surrounding her birth. Chief among them is getting stuck in traffic on the way to the hospital, forcing Robert to prepare to be Debra's midwife.

Memorable Moment: Ray: "Holy Moses . . . [then, to Robert] What are you looking at?"

Robert: "I'm waiting for the baby, Raymond."

Ray: "Your eyes gotta be so open?"

Air Date: May 21, 2001
Writer: Tucker Cawley
Director: Jerry Zaks
Guest Cast: Carey Eidel (Daddy), Jessica Bern (Nurse), Monique Edwards (Doctor)

SEASON 6

#123 THE ANGRY FAMILY

For his school presentation, Michael reads a story entitled "The Angry Family," leading the Barones to engage in furious finger-pointing over who is the cause.

Memorable Moment: Michael [reading]: "The Daddy was mad at the Mommy . . . the Mommy was mad at the Daddy . . . the Mommy and Daddy were very mad at the Grandpa . . . and Grandma got mad at everybody."

Air Date: September 24, 2001
Writer: Phil Rosenthal
Director: Gary Halvorson
Guest Cast: Charles Durning (Father Hubley), Elizabeth Anne Smith (Eileen), Richard Israel (Adam), Rhyon Nicole Brown (Gracie), Mitch Holleman (Ian)

#124 NO ROLL

Hoping to spice things up in the bedroom, Ray buys an adult board game, Sensuopoly.

Memorable Moment: Marie: "This game must be Debra's doing."

Ray: "Well, it's not."

Marie: "I should have guessed when I opened the fridge with two bottles of white wine. Are you swingers?"

Ray: "Alright, Mom, you just asked if I was a wife-swapper."

Frank: "Now there's an idea. I don't even have to swap. I'll just make a donation."

Air Date: October 1, 2001
Writer: Aaron Shure
Director: Jerry Zaks

#125 ODD MAN OUT

Marie begins giving Marco piano lessons and going to the opera with him, leading Frank and her to fight over him as a friend. Eventually, they force Marco to choose between them.

Memorable Moment: Marie wants to go to the opera. Frank: "Opera. Just what the world needs: more fat women screamin'."

Air Date: October 8, 2001
Writers: Steve Skrovan, Jeremy Stevens
Director: Jerry Zaks
Guest Cast: David Proval (Marco), Alex Meneses (Stefania), Fred Stoller (Gerard), Darlene Kardon (Aunt Gina)

#126 RAY'S RING

When Ray loses his wedding ring, he gets hit on by a woman in an airport.

Memorable Moment: Ray [to Debra]:

"Actually, it's a compliment to you. You're married to a very desirable man, honey bun. But the ladies can want me all they want, because [sings] 'There ain't no woman like the one I got.' [then] 'What? Where are you going?'"

Air Date: October 15, 2001
Writer: Mike Royce
Director: Kenneth R. Shapiro
Guest Cast: Jeff Garlin (Jimmy), Julie Claire (Alexis), Dianne Burnett (Woman), Ping Wu (Customer)

#127 MARIE'S SCULPTURE
Marie makes a sculpture in her art class and gives it to Ray and Debra. She considers it abstract, but no one wants to tell her what it obviously resembles.
Memorable Moment: Marie finally sees what everybody else sees. Marie: "Oh my God, I'm a lesbian."

Air Date: October 22, 2001
Writer: Jennifer Crittenden
Director: Randy Suhr
Guest Cast: Lauri Johnson (Sister Ann), Mary Gillis (Sister Beth), Rocky McMurray (Janitor)

#128 FRANK GOES DOWN-STAIRS
Ray and Debra fall out of bed during sex, causing minor injuries. Ray lies to Frank and says they fell down their stairs.
Memorable Moment: As Frank tries to fix Ray and Debra's stairs, he falls through them.
Marie: "Oh my God! Frank, are you alright?!"

Frank: "Holy crap."
Marie: "Don't move. I'm coming down."
Frank: "I'm in enough pain."

Air Date: October 29, 2001
Writer: Jennifer Crittenden
Director: Gary Halvorson
Guest Cast: Jon Manfrellotti (Gianni), Tom McGowan (Bernie), Richard Penn (Doctor)

#129 JEALOUS ROBERT
Debra and Marie plan to make Robert jealous by setting Amy up with Gianni, but their scheme backfires when Amy and Gianni hit it off.
Memorable Moment: Just before Ray can reveal Debra and Marie's plan to Robert, Debra elbows Ray accidentally, but directly, in the groin, causing him to crumple to the floor like a ton of bricks.

Air Date: November 5, 2001
Writers: Tom Caltabiano, Ray Romano
Director: Gary Halvorson
Guest Cast: Andy Kindler (Andy), Jon Manfrellotti (Gianni), Monica Horan (Amy)

#130 IT'S SUPPOSED TO BE FUN
At the kids' basketball game, Geoffrey overhears Ray making jokes about his poor play, which includes running around with his hands sticking out of the bottom of his shorts. Later, he tells Ray and Debra he doesn't want to play anymore, and nothing Ray says will convince him otherwise.
Memorable Moment: Ray greets Debra in the bedroom by entering with his hands sticking out of the bottom of his boxers, Geoffrey-style.

Air Date: November 12, 2001
Writer: Lew Schneider
Director: Gary Halvorson
Guest Cast: Dan Castellaneta (Bryan Trenberth), Heather McPhaul (Parent #1), Raymond Patterson (Parent #2), Todd Sandler (Referee), Nicolas Aranda (Kid #1)

#131 OLDER WOMEN
Debra's divorced parents are coming for Thanksgiving, and Warren is bringing a date. Everyone assumes she'll be some young floozy, but they are shocked when it turns out to be Emma, an elderly woman.
Memorable Moment: The family watches in silence as Emma takes an extremely long time climbing the stairs. When she finally reaches the top . . .
Frank: "Happy New Year."

Air Date: November 19, 2001
Writers: Tucker Cawley, Phil Rosenthal
Director: Gary Halvorson
Guest Cast: Robert Culp (Warren), Katherine Helmond (Lois), Patricia Place (Emma)

#132 RAYBERT
Robert has a problem: Natasha, the incredible woman he's dating, thinks he's Ray. Ray

makes Robert promise to tell her the truth, but then begins enjoying the vicarious thrill of people dating him through Robert.

Memorable Moment: Ray: "You know, it's like neither one of us could have gotten her on our own, but . . ."

Robert: "Melded together we were like a whole other . . . entity. Like a superhero. We were better than just Ray."

Ray: "Better than just Robert."

Robert: "We were . . . Raybert."

Air Date: November 26, 2001
Writer: Steve Skrovan
Director: Gary Halvorson
Guest Cast: Ana Ortiz (Natasha), Christine Gonzales (Wendi), Ruben Pla (Wendi's Father)

#133 THE KICKER

Frank catches a record-setting football while attending a college game with Robert, and he refuses to give it back to the kid who kicked it.

Memorable Moment: During the family's struggle to take the ball back from Frank, Robert ends up throwing it through Ray's living room window.

Air Date: December 10, 2001
Writer: Aaron Shure
Director: Gary Halvorson
Guest Cast: Scott St. James (Host), Boris Cabrera (Ron), Winston J. Rocha (Ron's Father), Hiram Kasten (Dave)

#134 SEASON'S GREETINGS

Debra is offended when Marie's Christmas letter includes veiled insults about her.

Memorable Moment: Robert writes his own section to be included in the new letter.

Ray [reading Robert's section]: "'Robert loves to dance and has been known to boogie the night away.' So let me get this straight. You broadened the definition of the term 'boogie' to include staying home by yourself eating Wheat Thins?"

Robert: "I am a dancer!"

Air Date: December 17, 2001
Writer: Tucker Cawley
Director: Jerry Zaks

#135 TISSUES

Ray is sick of Debra making every decision in the house, so she agrees to let him have more say. After Ray does some shopping and Debra questions his choice of tissues, Ray gets angry, then accidentally puts a box of the tissues near a burner on the stove, setting the kitchen on fire.

Memorable Moment: During the fire, Ray runs out and gets the hose. Unfortunately, it is a hose he bought. It's way too short, and the water won't reach the flames.
Air Date: January 7, 2002
Writer: Mike Royce
Director: Jerry Zaks
Guest Cast: Mark E. Smith (Contractor)

#136 SNOW DAY

The power goes out, and Ray and Debra are forced to spend the night at Frank and Marie's. Debra offends Frank by saying she can't believe she's actually having fun with him.

Memorable Moment: Ray [to Debra]: "You don't think you're better? You're not better than Frank Barone? You think that my father, a known baboon's ass, is your equal?"

Air Date: January 14, 2002
Writer: Kathy Ann Stumpe
Director: Gary Halvorson
Guest Cast: Monica Horan (Amy)

#137 COOKIES

Ally's troop leader, Peggy, takes a dislike to Ray, and the feeling is mutual. Later, Ray has Ally sell cookies in Peggy's prime spot, leading to a fight between Ray and Peggy that Debra has to break up.

Memorable Moment: Debra [to Peggy]: "Nobody beats up my husband!"

Air Date: January 28, 2002
Writer: Steve Skrovan
Director: Gary Halvorson
Guest Cast: Amy Aquino (Peggy), Arnetia Walker (Friendly Mom), Stephanie Courtney (Woman), Timmy Deters (Child), Hunter Grey (Frontier Girl), Nicholas DiNardo (Young Mook)

#138 LUCKY SUIT

Marie ruins Robert's suit jacket before his big interview for a job with the FBI, then, to make matters worse, she faxes a long apology

to the FBI agent who is interviewing him.

Memorable Moment: Robert squirms in embarrassment as the agent reads Marie's fax.

Agent Garfield [reading]: "Please ask Robert to forgive me. I tried, but it'll mean more coming from you." [then, to Robert] "Please forgive your mother."

Air Date: February 4, 2002
Writer: Tucker Cawley
Director: Gary Halvorson
Guest Cast: Sam Anderson (Agent Garfield), Carole Gutierrez (Secretary), Brooks Gardner (TV Voice)

#139 THE SKIT

For Lee and Stan's anniversary party, Ray and Debra do a skit that spoofs Frank and Marie, and, to Robert's surprise, his parents love it. Later, Frank and Marie imitate Ray and Debra, who don't take it nearly as well.

Memorable Moment: Frank imitates Ray as a "whiny needy baby," and Marie imitates Debra as a tarted-up sexpot.

Air Date: February 25, 2002
Writer: Lew Schneider
Director: Gary Halvorson
Guest Cast: Victor Raider-Wexler (Stan), Debra Mooney (Lee), Len Lesser (Garvin)

#140 THE BREAKUP TAPE

Debra finds an answering machine tape with a message from an old girlfriend breaking up with Ray. He then becomes jealous when he discovers that their house is filled with mementos from Debra's old boyfriends.

Memorable Moment: Ray reading a poem he has written for Debra, "Debra's Ears": "One

on each side like a dainty cup. / So gently they hold thine sunglasses up. / So round and nice with a subtle ridge / There's no bone in there, it's cartilage."

Air Date: March 4, 2002
Writers: Tom Caltabiano, Aaron Shure
Director: Jerry Zaks

#141 TALK TO YOUR DAUGHTER

Ray gives Ally a sex-ed talk, but Ally says she knows *how* we get here. She wants to know *why* we're here.

Memorable Moment: Robert declares that he has spent many a night in bed pondering life's imponderables.

Frank: "You need to find yourself a broad, and pronto."

Air Date: March 18, 2002
Writers: Tucker Cawley, Ray Romano
Director: Jerry Zaks
Guest Cast: Jon Manfrellotti (Gianni), Tom McGowan (Bernie)

#142 A VOTE FOR DEBRA

Debra runs for president of the school board, but she loses by six votes. Ray is glad she didn't lose by one, because he voted for one of her opponents.

Memorable Moment: Debra: "You were stuffing your pants with meat!"

Ray: "I'm your husband, you're supposed to support me no matter what's in my pants!"

Air Date: March 25, 2002
Writers: Lew Schneider, Steve Skrovan
Director: Jerry Zaks
Guest Cast: David Hunt (Parker), Elizabeth Herring (Carrie), Kevin Brief (Principal),

Kyra Groves (Woman), Jerry Lambert (Guy), Missy Doty (Mom #1), Adrienne Alitowski (Mom #2)

#143 THE FIRST SIX YEARS

Highlights from the first six seasons. They're all supposed to be memorable moments.

Air Date: April 28, 2002
Writer: Tony Desena
Director: Kenneth R. Shapiro

#144 CALL ME MOM

Marie wants Ray to stop calling Debra's mother "Mom." When Ray stops, Debra knows Marie is to blame. Ray then points out that Debra doesn't call Marie "Mom."

Memorable Moment: Debra tries calling Marie "Mom."

Marie: "You don't have to do that, dear."

Air Date: April 29, 2002
Writers: George B. White III, Joe Rubin
Director: Kenneth R. Shapiro
Guest Cast: Katherine Helmond (Lois)

#145 MOTHER'S DAY

Debra loses her temper with Marie and refuses to apologize, which leads to a standoff.

Memorable Moment: Ray: "Come on, it's Mother's Day. Can't one of you two mothers just say somethin'?"

Air Date: May 6, 2002
Writer: Jennifer Crittenden
Director: Gary Halvorson
Guest Cast: Anne Gee Byrd (Hilda), Fred Ornstein (Artie)

#146 THE BIGGER PERSON

Debra and Marie are still fighting, so Ray and his father decide to pit Marie and Debra against each other for their own gain.

Memorable Moment: Robert: "By God, I'll do whatever it takes to make this family whole!"

Ray: "I think you're the family hole."

Air Date: May 13, 2002
Writers: Tucker Cawley, Lew Schneider
Director: Gary Halvorson

#147 THE FIRST TIME

In a flashback to fifteen years earlier, Marie, Frank, Robert, and an unwitting Father Hubley interrupt Ray and Debra's date to stop them from having sex.

Memorable Moment: Debra [realizing Marie's plan]: "Is that why you're all here? Because of sex?"

Father Hubley: "I was only told about the lasagna."

Air Date: May 20, 2002
Writers: Tom Caltabiano, Mike Royce, Ray Romano
Director: Gary Halvorson
Guest Cast: Charles Durning (Father Hubley), Jon Manfrellotti (Gianni), Tom McGowan (Bernie)

SEASON 7

#148 THE CULT

When a giddy Robert tells the family that he has joined a group called Inner Path, Marie fears he has joined a cult.

Memorable Moment: Robert: "It's not a cult! It's just a bunch of people who want to see me

happy and who happen to care about me."

Marie: "You have that here, you stupid ass!"

Air Date: September 23, 2002
Writers: Phil Rosenthal, Tucker Cawley
Director: Kenneth R. Shapiro
Guest Cast: Fred Stoller (Gerard), Sherri Shepherd (Judy), Susan Yeagley (Mariann)

#149 COUNSELLING

When Debra finds out that Bernie and Linda have been going to marriage counselling and are getting results, she makes an appointment for her and Ray to go.

Memorable Moment: Debra: "Well, just as an example, last week Ray came home late from golfing, and I guess golf is a hot button issue with me, and we had a fight.

Pamela: "Ray, do you remember this?"

Ray: "I do. I shot a ninety-four."

Air Date: September 30, 2002
Writer: Mike Royce
Director: Kenneth R. Shapiro
Guest Cast: Tom McGowan (Bernie), Maggie Wheeler (Linda), Nancy Lenehan (Pamela)

#150 HOMEWORK

After telling Ally's teacher that she has too much homework, Ray has to suggest changes to the school board. Marie has to help him and blows a fuse, hearing Ray's use of language.

Memorable Moment: Marie: "You do not end a sentence with 'at.'"

Ray: "Alright, big deal, I ended it with a proposition."

Marie: "Preposition. It's a prep—oh my God!"

Ray: "What? What are you so upset about?"

Marie: "Because this is the end of civilization!"

Air Date: October 7, 2002
Writer: Jeremy Stevens
Director: Gary Halvorson
Guest Cast: Kimberly Scott (Miss Purcell), Julie Dretziin (Mother #1), Lynn Tufeld (Mother #2), Diana Tanaka (Ms. Silber), Jerry Lambert (Guy), Henry LeBlanc (Board Member #1)

#151 PET THE BUNNY

Ray has written a eulogy for Frank that includes his childhood memory of Frank petting a bunny. Frank denies it ever happened.

Memorable Moment: Frank: "I'm the tough guy! That's how the community sees me!"

Ray: "What community? You're in a steam room at the lodge with six naked guys."

Air Date: October 14, 2002
Writer: Aaron Shure
Director: John Fortenberry
Guest Cast: Victor Raider-Wexler (Stan), Len Lesser (Garvin)

#152 WHO AM I?

After a lame night with the guys, Ray gets confused about who he is and decides to spend some time at Frank's lodge.

Memorable Moment: When Debra takes Ray to hear an author speak at a bookstore, he falls asleep, prompting her to wake him with an elbow to the eye.

Air Date: October 21, 2002

Writer: David Regal
Director: John Fortenberry
Guest Cast: Jon Manfrellotti (Gianni), Tom McGowan (Bernie), Maggie Wheeler (Linda), Victor Raider-Wexler (Stan), Len Lesser (Garvin), Max Rosenthal (Max), Albert Romano (Albert), J. G. Hertzler (Everett), James Rich (Brian)

#153 ROBERT NEEDS MONEY

After hearing about his financial struggles, Ray and Debra give Robert a thousand dollars. The next day, Robert says that thanks to them, he's going to Las Vegas!

Memorable Moment: Robert: "Come on, Ray. The Barone brothers on the Strip."

Ray: "No, I can't go there. I'll go one day, probably ten years from now to drag Ally out of a casino chapel."

Air Date: October 28, 2002
Writer: Tom Caltabiano
Director: Michael Zinberg

#154 THE SIGH

Ray and Debra are in their bathroom when he gets in her way. She sighs, and Ray suggests their bathroom should be just hers. Debra loves the idea and changes it into a paradise.

Memorable Moment: Shower spray fight!

Air Date: November 4, 2002
Writer: Steve Skrovan
Director: Jerry Zaks

―――――――

#155 THE ANNOYING KID

When Ray and Debra's new friends come over, their son, Spencer, jumps on the beds and uses refrigerator magnets to spell out "RAY STINKS."

Memorable Moment: Later, Marie discovers someone has spelled out "MARIE STINKS" on her refrigerator, and we hear Frank laugh.

Air Date: November 11, 2002
Writer: Lew Schneider
Director: Jerry Zaks
Guest Cast: Craig Anton (Neil), Cheryl Hines (Lauren), Brett Buford (Spencer)

―――――――

#156 SHE'S THE ONE

Robert's new girlfriend, Angela, comes over for dinner. She seems great—until Ray sees her eat a fly. He then tries to get Robert to believe what he saw.

Memorable Moment: Ray [horrified]: "She's not the one!"

Air Date: November 18, 2002
Writers: Ray Romano, Phil Rosenthal
Director: John Fortenberry
Guest Cast: Monica Horan (Amy), Elizabeth Bogush (Angela), Aaron D. Spears (Rick), Michael Papajohn (Waiter)

#157 MARIE'S VISION

Marie gets eyeglasses and can see Debra's thinning eyelashes, Ray's gray hair, and Robert's wrinkles.

Memorable Moment: Amy: "Your mother notices a few wrinkles on him, so he goes to some doctor in the yellow pages and paralyzes his face."

Robert: "It's tentarary."

Air Date: November 25, 2002
Writer: Jay Kogen
Director: Sheldon Epps
Guest Cast: Monica Horan (Amy)

―――――――

#158 THE THOUGHT THAT COUNTS

Debra asks Ray why he puts more thought into gifts for Marie than for her. Ray lies and says he already bought her something very special for Christmas.

Memorable Moment: The look on Robert's face as Debra is thrilled with her first edition copy of *To Kill a Mockingbird* . . . her very thoughtful gift from Ray, which was completely Robert's idea.

Air Date: December 9, 2002
Writer: Tucker Cawley
Director: Gary Halvorson
Guest Cast: Monica Horan (Amy)

#159 GRANDPA STEALS

In front of Ally, Frank gets accused of stealing at the grocery store and gets very angry with the produce man, Jimmy.

Memorable Moment: Frank, really wanting to throw a tomato at Jimmy, has to put it down.

Air Date: January 6, 2003
Writer: Lew Schneider
Director: Jerry Zaks
Guest Cast: Jeff Garlin (Jimmy)

#160 SOMEBODY HATES RAYMOND

Ray's friend Andy gets a job on a sports radio show hosted by Jerry Musso, but he tells Ray that he can't be on the show because . . . Jerry hates Ray.

Memorable Moment: Robert steps in to defend Ray against Jerry.

Air Date: January 27, 2003
Writer: Steve Skrovan
Director: Jerry Zaks
Guest Cast: Andy Kindler (Andy), Steve Vinovich (Jerry Musso)

#161 JUST A FORMALITY

When Robert asks Amy's parents for her hand in marriage, they very politely say no.

Memorable Moment: As snow falls on a city street, Robert gets down on one knee and proposes to Amy. Marie, bursting from a police car: "Yes! She said yes!"

Air Date: February 3, 2003
Writers: Phil Rosenthal, Steve Skrovan
Director: Gary Halvorson
Guest Cast: Monica Horan (Amy), Chris Elliott (Peter), Fred Willard (Hank), Georgia Engel (Pat), Dan Martin (Policeman #1), Richard Romano (Policeman #2)

#162 THE DISCIPLINARIAN

Debra tells Ray to stop being obsessed with wanting to be liked by the kids and puts him in charge of discipline. He goes overboard and bans TV for a month.

Memorable Moment: The family discovers that a topless photo of Debra was once in the newspaper.

Ray: "Found yourself on page seven of the *Daily News* with your boobs out."
Debra: "Ray!"
Frank: "Holy crap!"
Ray: "In the *Daily News*."
Debra: "I was not topless. They put a black bar over the exposed area."
Frank: "I hate those."

Air Date: February 10, 2003
Writer: Mike Royce
Director: Jerry Zaks

#163 SWEET CHARITY

Debra signs Ray up to volunteer at a hospital. He ends up loving it and spending more time there than at home, until one night he finds Robert has taken his place.

Memorable Moment: Ray tries to win back the stage from Robert and gets booed by an elderly woman.

Air Date: February 24, 2003
Writer: Aaron Shure
Director: Jerry Zaks

Guest Cast: Adrian Ricard (Lesley), Emy Coligado (Claudia), Tara Karsian (Jean), Donna Cooper (Beth), Betty Murphy (Margaret)

#164 MEETING THE PARENTS

When Amy's parents show up to discourage her from marrying Robert, they fight with the Barones about everything from muffins to God.

Memorable Moment: Frank calls Hank a liar. Frank: "See, Marie, I bet all his stuff about church was a load of crap, too. Probably spends all day Sunday watching TV in a muffin shop."
Hank: "You know what, Debra? I will pray. [to Frank] For you."
Frank: "Oh, no. You don't pray for me, pal. I pray for you!"

Air Date: February 17, 2003
Writers: Mike Royce, Lew Schneider
Director: Jerry Zaks
Guest Cast: Monica Horan (Amy), Chris Elliott (Peter), Fred Willard (Hank), Georgia Engel (Pat)

#165 THE PLAN

Ray helps Robert write a wedding invitation so terrible that Amy will never ask Robert to do anything again. The invitations get sent out by mistake, and Amy thinks Robert doesn't want to get married.

Memorable Moment: Debra accuses Ray of faking different things throughout their marriage. Debra: "Then explain to me how you can't fold a shirt?! Explain to me how an adult human with thumbs is not able to do that!"

Ray: "I don't know. It's embarrassing."

Debra: "Uh-huh. Yeah. What else? What else have you faked?"

Ray: "Nothing, Debra, come on!"

Debra: "The bed!"

Ray: "Now wait a minute. That's one place I always give a hundred and ten percent."

Debra: "I mean making the bed!"

Air Date: March 17, 2003
Writer: Tucker Cawley
Director: Jerry Zaks
Guest Cast: Monica Horan (Amy), Fred Willard (Hank), Georgia Engel (Pat)

#166 SLEEPOVER AT PEGGY'S

Ray quickly assembles a tent for some kids at a sleepover Ally is attending at her friend Molly's. Molly's mom, Peggy, thanks him with a pat on the rump, and he wonders if she was coming on to him.

Memorable Moment: In the spirit of investigation, Ray pats Robert's behind just as Debra walks down the stairs.

Air Date: March 24, 2003
Writers: Joe Rubin, George B. White III
Director: Gary Halvorson
Guest Cast: Jon Manfrellotti (Gianni), Amy Aquino (Peggy), Alexandra Romano (Molly)

#167 WHO'S NEXT

When Rose Caputo, the woman Marie had chosen to take care of Frank if he were to outlive her, dies, Ray and Debra pick replacement spouses for each other.

Memorable Moment: After Debra reveals she would pick her cute friend Linda to be with Ray . . . Debra: "You're picturing her naked, aren't you?"

Ray: "No, no, no . . . no."

Debra: "I know she has a good body."

Ray: "She does? Well, I never noticed."

Debra: "Oh, you are so full of it. I'm not even dead yet, you're already fantasizing about having sex with Linda!"

Air Date: April 14, 2003
Story: Miriam Trogdon
Writer: Steve Skrovan
Director: Gary Halvorson
Guest Cast: Monica Horan (Amy), Tom McGowan (Bernie), Maggie Wheeler (Linda), Ralph Monaco (George), Renata Scott (Harriet), Joe Durrenberger (Funeral Director)

#168 THE SHOWER

After sleeping "drunk" behind the wheel, Debra spends a night in jail, temporarily loses her driver's license and is forced to rely on Marie.

Memorable Moment: Robert seeing Debra behind bars. Robert: ". . . Debra?"

Debra: "Hi, Robert."

Robert: "Oh my God. She finally killed Mom."

Air Date: April 28, 2003
Writer: Leslie Caveny
Director: Jerry Zaks
Guest Cast: Monica Horan (Amy), Sherri

Shepherd (Judy), Georgia Engel (Pat), Joel Brooks (Mr. Rodell), Billy Mayo (Officer Keon), Carmen Vargas (Guard), Maureen Da Rosa (Co-Ed)

#169 BAGGAGE

There's a suitcase sitting at the foot of the stairs from Ray and Debra's vacation two weeks ago. He hasn't moved it. She hasn't moved it. Neither has said a word, and they know they're waiting each other out.

Memorable Moment: Marie tells Debra the story of why the big fork and spoon have been hanging on her kitchen wall for forty-five years.

Marie: "Trust me, dear, it's not worth it. Go. Go move the luggage. You be the better person, hmm? Don't let a suitcase filled with cheese be your big fork and spoon."

Air Date: May 5, 2003
Writer: Tucker Cawley
Director: Gary Halvorson

#170 THE BACHELOR PARTY

After a lame bachelor party at Robert's apartment, Ray throws Robert a surprise bachelor

party at the lodge, which is a disaster, too.

Memorable Moment: Ray and Robert come home a little tipsy to find Debra, Amy, and Marie in the kitchen.

Debra: "So what did you guys do?"

Robert [to Amy, smiling]: "Enough talking. Maybe you should take me home."

Amy: "Oh my."

Marie: "I bet there were strippers. Were there strippers?"

Ray: "No, that's why we're here."

Debra: "Oh God, every woman's dream."

Marie: "I can only imagine what's waiting for me at home. [She thinks about it, then] Goodnight." [She rushes out.]

Air Date: May 12, 2003
Writers: Tom Caltabiano, Ray Romano, Mike Royce
Director: Gary Halvorson
Guest Cast: Monica Horan (Amy), Chris Elliott (Peter), Fred Willard (Hank), Andy Kindler (Andy), Jon Manfrellotti (Gianni), Tom McGowan (Bernie), Len Lesser (Garvin), Victor Raider-Wexler (Stan), Fred Stoller (Gerard), Max Rosenthal (Max), Albert Romano (Albert), Richard Romano (Rich)

#171 ROBERT'S WEDDING

Marie interrupts Robert and Amy's vows. From the altar, Robert tells her she's ruined every big event in his life. At the reception, Frank fights with Hank over the cash bar, and Pat, very sweetly, tells off Marie.

Memorable Moment: Ray comes up with a toast to Robert and Amy, advising them to edit their memories of their marriage. . . . Then, Robert and Amy have their first dance.

Air Date: May 19, 2003

Writer: Phil Rosenthal
Director: Jerry Zaks
Guest Cast: Monica Horan (Amy), Fred Willard (Hank), Georgia Engel (Pat), Chris Elliott (Peter), Jon Manfrellotti (Gianni), Chelcie Ross (Reverend Stevens), John C. McDonnell (DJ), Dan Kinsella (Bartender), Andy Kindler (Andy), Tom McGowan (Bernie), Maggie Wheeler (Linda), Fred Stoller (Gerard), Sherri Shepherd (Judy), Dan Martin (Policeman)

SEASON 8

#172 FUN WITH DEBRA

Debra wants to recapture the fun of their dating days and talks Ray into taking her golfing.

Memorable Moment: Ray: "Listen, golf . . . golf is . . . it's a frustrating game. And . . . and it's really hot out there. And . . . and if there's lightning, you could be killed. Alright. Listen. . . . If . . . if you want to go golfing [long silence] we'll go, because you're my girlfriend. And if there's lightning, I'll just step in front of you and take it in the head."

Air Date: September 22, 2003
Writer: Mike Scully
Director: Gary Halvorson
Guest Cast: Steven Hack (Arthur)

#173 THANK YOU NOTES

When Marie mentions to Amy that nobody has received thank you notes for their wedding gifts, Amy says she'll get to it when she can and causes their first fight. Debra is inspired and encourages Amy to join forces with her to remove Marie from power.

Memorable Moment: Debra fights hard to

keep Amy from giving in to Marie's manipulation, but ultimately loses. Debra [about Amy, sadly]: "She's gone."

Air Date: September 29, 2003
Writer: Phil Rosenthal
Director: Kenneth R. Shapiro
Guest Cast: Monica Horan (Amy), Debra Mooney (Lee)

#174 HOME FROM SCHOOL

Ray has to work from home because Michael won't go to school, and is annoyed with his son until he finds out the real reason the boy wants to stay home.

Memorable Moment: Ray tells Michael the story about when he wet himself on the baseball field and was dubbed "Pee Pee Raymond."

Air Date: October 6, 2003
Writer: Steve Skrovan
Director: Kenneth R. Shapiro
Guest Cast: Daryl Sabara (Kid)

#175 MISERY LOVES COMPANY

Ray and Debra take offense when Robert and Amy offer them relationship advice after just three months of marriage.

Memorable Moment: Marie gives her own marriage advice to the couples.

Amy: "But Marie, you said 'hate.' How can hate have any place in a marriage?"

Marie: "You make room. There's gonna be hate. Hate is real. Marriage is real. We might fight, but . . . we're okay with each other, and do you know why? We've endured. We have been through it all . . . and now . . ."

Frank: "We're waiting for death."

Air Date: October 13, 2003
Writer: Aaron Shure
Director: Gary Halvorson
Guest Cast: Monica Horan (Amy)

#176 THE CONTRACTOR

Debra wants a new stove, so she and Ray hire Gianni to install it.

Memorable Moment: Gianni repeatedly, and more forcefully each time, tries to force the stove into place.

Air Date: October 20, 2003
Writer: Mike Royce
Director: Gary Halvorson
Guest Cast: Monica Horan (Amy), Jon Manfrellotti (Gianni)

#177 PETER ON THE COUCH

When Amy's brother, Peter, outstays his welcome on her and Robert's couch, Ray is forced to drive Peter back home to Pennsylvania, where he is shocked to find that his parents are turning his room into a Bible study.

Memorable Moment: Peter finds out that his parents have been keeping his cat outside.

Peter: "What? Outside?! No! Miss Puss is an inside cat!"

Pat: "Not anymore."

Air Date: November 3, 2003
Writer: Steven James Meyer
Director: Gary Halvorson
Guest Cast: Monica Horan (Amy), Fred Willard (Hank), Georgia Engel (Pat), Chris Elliott (Peter)

#178 LIARS

In an attempt to cover a little white lie Ray told Marie, Debra and Ray are forced to tell one bigger lie after another, until they have both gotten so good at it that neither one is sure they can trust the other.

Memorable Moment: Marie catches the scent that Ray and Debra have been lying to her.

Marie [pulling Ray aside]: "What is the name of the hotel? Ah, wait, wait, wait. Why don't you whisper the name to me, and then we'll see what Debra says it is. Come over here. Come on. Go ahead."

Ray [loud whisper as he looks at Debra]: "Ra-ma-da."

Air Date: November 10, 2003
Writer: Tucker Cawley
Director: Kenneth R. Shapiro
Guest Cast: Monica Horan (Amy), Alexandra Romano (Molly)

#179 THE SURPRISE PARTY

Lois tells Ray of her plan to throw a surprise birthday party for Debra. When Ray accidentally leaks the idea to Debra, she assumes he's the one throwing the party and is so touched that he allows her to believe it.

Memorable Moment: The look on Debra's face when Ray whispers to her that everybody at her party knows that she knows about the surprise.

Air Date: November 17, 2003
Writer: Lew Schneider
Director: Jerry Zaks
Guest Cast: Monica Horan (Amy), Katherine Helmond (Lois), Maggie Wheeler (Linda), Christopher T. Wood (Waiter #1), Michael Duddie (Waiter #2)

#180 THE BIRD

The Barones go to Pennsylvania for Thanksgiving. All is going fine until Pat puts a wounded bird out of its misery.

Memorable Moment: Ray confronts Peter during the Thanksgiving pageant, rips off his shirt, and proclaims, "I'm Squanto!"

Air Date: November 24, 2003
Writers: Tucker Cawley, Mike Royce, Jeremy Stevens
Director: Kenneth R. Shapiro
Guest Cast: Monica Horan (Amy), Fred Willard (Hank), Georgia Engel (Pat), Chris Elliott (Peter)

#181 JAZZ RECORDS

After being reminded that he ruined Frank's favorite jazz records long ago, a guilt-ridden Ray tries to replace the albums with CDs. But Frank isn't satisfied. He wants his old records.

Memorable Moment: Robert enters Frank and Marie's living room, slipping, falling, and finally landing on their holiday shopping bags.

Robert: "What am I sitting in?"
Marie: "Eggs. And eggnog."
Robert: "And what is very sharp?"
Frank: "That might be the menorah."
Robert: "The menorah?"
Frank: "It was a big sale."

Air Date: December 15, 2003
Writer: Tom Caltabiano
Director: Gary Halvorson

Episode guide complete through December 15, 2003

AWARDS & HONORS

2003

PRIMETIME EMMY AWARDS
Everybody Loves Raymond, Outstanding Comedy Series (*above*)

Brad Garrett, Outstanding Supporting Actor in a Comedy Series

Doris Roberts, Outstanding Supporting Actress in a Comedy Series

Tucker Cawley, Outstanding Writing for a Comedy Series

Everybody Loves Raymond, Outstanding Multi-Camera Sound Mixing for a Series or Special

AFI AWARDS
Everybody Loves Raymond, Television Program of the Year

AMERICAN WOMEN IN RADIO AND TELEVISION (AWRT) GRACIE ALLEN AWARD
Patricia Heaton, Lead Actor, Comedy

GOLDEN SATELLITE AWARDS
Doris Roberts, Best Performance by an Actress in a Series, Comedy, or Musical

PEOPLE'S CHOICE AWARDS
Ray Romano, Favorite Male Television Performer

SCREEN ACTORS GUILD (SAG) AWARDS
Peter Boyle, Brad Garrett, Patricia Heaton, Doris Roberts, Ray Romano, Madylin Sweeten, Outstanding Performance by an Ensemble in a Comedy Series

2002

PRIMETIME EMMY AWARDS
Ray Romano, Outstanding Lead Actor in a Comedy Series

Brad Garrett, Outstanding Supporting Actor in a Comedy Series

Doris Roberts, Outstanding Supporting Actress in a Comedy Series

PEOPLE'S CHOICE AWARDS
Ray Romano, Favorite Male Television Performer

WRITERS GUILD AWARDS (WGA)
Philip Rosenthal, "Italy Parts 1 & 2," Episodic Comedy

2001

PRIMETIME EMMY AWARDS
Patricia Heaton, Outstanding Lead Actress in a Comedy Series

Doris Roberts, Outstanding Supporting Actress in a Comedy Series

Everybody Loves Raymond, Outstanding Multi-Camera Sound Mixing for a Series or Special

AMERICAN COMEDY AWARDS
Everybody Loves Raymond, Funniest Television Series

AWRT GRACIE ALLEN AWARD
Everybody Loves Raymond

HUMANITAS PRIZE
Jennifer Crittenden, "Ray's Journal," Humanitas Prize for Half-Hour Primetime Network, Syndicated, or Cable

TV GUIDE AWARDS
Everybody Loves Raymond, Comedy Series of the Year

Ray Romano, Actor of the Year in a Comedy Series

Doris Roberts, Supporting Actress of the Year in a Comedy Series

2000

PRIMETIME EMMY AWARDS
Patricia Heaton, Outstanding Actress in a Comedy Series

AMERICAN COMEDY AWARDS
Ray Romano, Funniest Male Performer in a Television Series, Leading Role

RELIGION COMMUNICATORS COUNCIL WILBUR AWARDS
Everybody Loves Raymond, Best Television Comedy

TV GUIDE AWARDS
Everybody Loves Raymond, Favorite Comedy Series *(below)*

AWRT GRACIE ALLEN AWARD
Everybody Loves Raymond—"Working Girl"

VIEWERS FOR QUALITY TELEVISION
Everybody Loves Raymond, Best Quality Comedy Series

Patricia Heaton, Best Actress in a Quality Comedy Series

Ray Romano, Best Actor in a Quality Comedy Series

Doris Roberts, Best Supporting Actress in a Quality Comedy Series

1999

AMERICAN COMEDY AWARDS
Doris Roberts, Funniest Female Performance in a Television Series

TELEVISION CRITICS ASSOCIATION (TCA)
Ray Romano, Outstanding Individual Achievement in Comedy

VIEWERS FOR QUALITY TELEVISION
Everybody Loves Raymond, Best Quality Comedy Series

Patricia Heaton, Best Actress in a Quality Comedy Series

Ray Romano, Best Actor in a Quality Comedy Series

Doris Roberts, Best Supporting Actress in a Quality Comedy Series

1998

VIEWERS FOR QUALITY TELEVISION
Doris Roberts, Best Supporting Actress in a Quality Comedy Series

YOUNG ARTIST AWARDS
Madylin Sweeten, Best Performance in a TV Comedy Series, Young Actress Age Ten or Under

BACKSTAGE
STAFF & CREW

Executive Producer: Phil Rosenthal
Assistant to Mr. Rosenthal: Erin Champion

Executive Producer: Ray Romano
Assistant to Mr. Romano: Christy Kallhovd

Executive Producer: Stu Smiley
Executive Producer: Rory Rosegarten
Assistant to Mr. Rosegarten: Brian Friedman

Executive Producer: Lew Schneider
Executive Producer: Tucker Cawley
Executive Producer: Steve Skrovan
Executive Producer: Jeremy Stevens
Co-Executive Producer: Lisa Helfrich Jackson
Co-Executive Producer: Tom Caltabiano
Co-Executive Producer: Aaron Shure
Co-Executive Producer: Mike Scully
Co-Executive Producer: Mike Royce
Supervising Producer: Leslie Caveny
Producer: Holli Gailen
Producer/UPM: Ken Ornstein

Directors: Gary Halvorson, Jerry Zaks,
   Kenneth R. Shapiro, Brian Roberts
Writers' Assistants: Steve Meyer, Frank Pines
Writers' Assistants/P.A.s: Simon Brown,
   Tim Peach
Writers' P.A.: George B. White III

PRODUCTION
1st Assistant Director: Randy Suhr
2nd Assistant Director: Elena Santaballa
Script Supervisor: Ellen Halpin
Production Supervisor: Kevin O'Donnell
Assistant Production Coordinator: Amy Janon
Production Secretary: Meg Schave
Production Assistants: Mike Pines, Chad Silver

ACCOUNTING
Production Accountant: Vicki Carnall
Assistant Accountant: Terry Cole
Assistant Accountant: Wendy Hyden

STAND-INS
Ray: Wolfgang Track
Patty: Sarah Hale
Doris: Maya Bond
Peter: Mike Duddie
Brad: Joe Durrenberger
Madylin: Susie Rossito
Additional Cast: Carmen Vargas

Studio Teacher: Arlene Singer-Gross
Studio Teacher: Maura Gannett
Technical Coordinator: Kenneth R. Shapiro

Audience Switcher: Christine Ballard
Dialogue Coach: Elizabeth Herring

CASTING
Casting Director: Lisa Miller Katz
Casting Associate: Maggie Sherman

CAMERA
Director of Photography: Mike Berlin
Camera Operators: Tim Tyler (A Cam), Cary
McCrystal (B Cam), Paul Basta (C Cam),
Irv Waitsman (X Cam)

1st Assistant Camera: David Dechant (A Cam),
John Graham (B Cam), Jeff Goldenberg (C
Cam), Ed Natividad (X Cam)

2nd Assistant Camera: Steve Masias
Video Utility: Matt Minkoff, Scott Spiegel

ELECTRIC
Gaffer: Bill Fine
Best Boy: Kenneth Mann
Dimmerboard Operator: Mark Engel
Electricians: Sylvester Stewart, George Fundora

GRIP
Key Grip: Jim Dunn
Best Boy: Burt Poehlman
Dolly Grips: Ed Zaffina (A Cam), Peter Van
   Eynde (B Cam), Leandra Lack (C Cam),
   Basil Schmidt (X Cam)
Grips: Bill Flemming, Jr., Bruce Alexander

SOUND
Sound Mixer: Brentley Walton
A2/Recordist: Billy Youdelman
Boom Operators: Dave Stafford, Tim Fistler
Sound Utility: Jim Norris, Wilfred Whyle

ART DEPT.
Art Director: Sharon Busse
Assistant Art Director: L. J. Houdyshell
Set Decorator: Donna Stamps
Leadman: Dan Dupont
Set Dressers: Judson Crowder, Michael
   Parianos, Steven Watson

CONSTRUCTION
Construction Coordinator: Roger Janson
Construction Foreman: Bob Perry
Carpenter: Doug Canvanaugh
Painters: Kelly Hudson, Mary Janson
Laborer: Terry MacDonald

TRANSPORTATION
Transportation Captain: Buddy Regan
Driver (Set Dressing): Eric Learnard

PROPERTY
Property Master: Rhonda Robinson
Assistant Property Master: Don Rosemond

CRAFT SERVICE
Craft Service: Larry Babitz

WARDROBE
Costume Designer: Simon Tuke
Costume Supervisor: Ashley Steuer
Key Costumer: Sonya Frisiner
Costumer: Mary Ellen Bosche

MAKEUP/HAIR
Key Makeup Artist: Shelly Woodhouse-Collins
Makeup Artist: Christine Steele
Key Hair Stylist: Ralph Albalos
Hair Stylist: Troy Zestos

AUDIENCE WARM-UP
Audience Warm-Up: Mark Sweet

POST-PRODUCTION
Editor: Pat Barnett
Composer: Rick Marotta
Post-Production Assistant: Maureen Da Rosa
Digitizer: Nickolas Perry

as of December 2003